JUICY 2: GETTING EVEN

Nicety

Copyright © 2013 **Black Cherry Publishing**

Facebook: nicetycouture

Twitter: @NicetyCouture

Website: www.nicetyzone.com

YouTube: mswordpoison

Instagram: iamnicety

ACKNOWLEDGEMENTS

Giving honor to God; who is the head of my household. Thank you to my family; I will love you all until the end of time, you are the air that I breathe.

To my friends; thanks for keeping me afloat when I thought I would sink.

To my fans and many followers; I love you all more than words can say. Thank you for the love and support you deliver each day!

DEDICATION

Aside from the normal dedications that I do to
everyone I know, I would like to dedicate this
book to one special woman. You believed in me,
inspired me, and never put my work down.
You supported me, encouraged me, and always
and always turned my frown upside down.
Gone too soon but never forgotten.

Blessed in Paradise,

Earline Hannon-Webster

JUICY 2:
GETTING EVEN

Chapter 1: "Why do you want me so bad? I'm not as perfect as you think I am." – *Pandora*

"Chow time, line up!" The Cook County correctional officer yelled as he guards the food service attendants at their carts.

"I'm so sick of this disgusting ass shit they choose to serve us every day." Pandora snarled as she lines up to receive her lunch tray. "You'd think after 3 weeks in this shit hole I'd be used to it by now, but all I want to do is haul it across the room at those black uniform wearing assholes."

"You say something Ms. Burden?" the officer yelled from across the room.

"No sir," Pandora grits her teeth in response.

She shook her head knowing that the only reason why the officers kept fucking with her was because of that stunt she pulled when she first got arrested. All she could think about was if she had succeeded in killing herself, she would not be dealing with the bullshit. Ever since then, the officers have been taunting her, teasing her, and fucking with her for no reason. They don't like it when you fuck with one of their own, in any way, period. They had a low tolerance for dumb shit and Pandora had started off on the wrong foot displaying that she was capable of pulling it at a moment's notice. The officers made sure to keep an extra eye locked on her.

"Simple motherfucka," Pandora barked quietly.

"Shut the fuck up girl. Damn, all I've heard you do is complain for these past two weeks and I swear I'm sick of it," Oxy snapped, slightly leaning back to give her a glimpse of the pissed look she had on her face.

Pandora took the blue tray that was handed to her of a single serving fruit punch juice box; a tossed together thick breaded grilled cheese and mystery meat sandwich and an apple. The sight of it made her gag and her hunger pangs nearly ceased. Every time they served the sandwiches it made her stay on the steel seat-less toilet for days. She side eyed Oxy as she walked ahead of her for her remark. To Pandora, it did not seem like all she did was complained, but she needed to vent to somebody and since Oxy was her cellmate, she figured what better person to listen than her.

Oxy was seated at a table alone when Pandora sat down at the same table across from her. She could read the annoyance written all over her face and chose to eat her lunch in silence rather than ruffle her feathers any longer. Even though Oxy was the first person to befriend her since she arrived, the girl had a mean streak. She was known to put bitches in their place regardless of how they or anyone else felt about it. Pandora got lucky that on the day she came to bunk in her cell with her, Oxy was in a good mood and very talkative.

A bad girl most of her 19 years of living, Oxy was a tall, rough neck girl with a bad attitude who was in for unlawful use of a weapon. Her fascination with guns stemmed from watching her dad take apart and put together his guns all the time. He was an army man making her the perfect army brat but she went rogue once her mother left them for another man. Oxy's whole outlook on life changed in an instant at the tender age of 14, jumping in and out of Juvenile Detention, fighting, and drinking heavily with drugs. Now that she was a grown woman in the eyes of the law, hard time in a real prison seemed to be her future.

Pandora stared at the long scar on Oxy's face. It curled from behind her ear and made its way to the crack of her mouth. It was heeled but it was dark and slightly rose causing anyone in its path to stop and stare. Pandora tried not to stare when Oxy was looking though. It ticked her off too much when people examined her like some sort of freak of nature. Her short buzz cut and rough demeanor made her resemble a boy, but her blue eyes, Caucasian tanned skin and awkwardly thin lips coupled with her high cheek bones made her look very feminine. Her feminine traits were what Oxy hated the most. Since girly looking Pandora showed up in her cell she had been working out doing pushups three times a day in order to bulk up past her frail looking stature.

"What are you looking at?" Oxy snarled looking up at Pandora while she munched on her lunch.

"Nothing, I was just trying to figure out what snake crawled up your butt today."

"Man, why something gotta be wrong with me? You the one with the issues," Oxy ripped open her juice box and threw its contents to the back of her throat, "Let's just drop it."

"Have you talked to your Public Defender yet?" Pandora asked nibbling at her choke sandwich.

"Naw that motherfucka don't give a fuck about me, and he ain't getting any money for this shit. I don't give a fuck. I know I'll be here for minute."

"Well, I talked to mine yesterday. He said

the judge wouldn't decrease my bail. So I gotta post up for two more weeks until my court date," Pandora shook her head, "If I had the money to get a decent fucking lawyer, I wouldn't even be in this hell hole."

"Yeah, I feel you. My dad wants to bail me out, but I won't accept his calls. I'm not ready to face him yet after running out on him two years ago. Now he just checks the county periodically to see if I'm here to try to contact me."

"Shit, I wouldn't give a fuck. Anything is better than this. If he loves you enough to hunt you down like that you should call him."

"Naw, our relationship is more complicated than you think. I can't do that right now." Oxy shook her head.

"I wish I had an old man to get me out of this mess my bitch ass sisters put me in. Those hoes should be sitting right here with me. They are just as guilty as I am."

"Have you ever tried taking some fucking responsibility for your own damn actions? Maybe you should stop to think about what you have done to get yourself in this shit in the first place. I can own up to my shit, you need to own up to yours." Oxy barked before snatching up her tray to toss in the garbage and leaving the table.

Pandora looked on in complete shock; she wondered what brought on the sudden urge for Oxy dumping on her. The entire time that they had been cellmates she had always listened to her problems, never giving an ounce of negativity or advice for that matter. But now she was dishing out a dose of reality that Pandora was not ready to handle. It seemed now that her thinking was premature but she considered her to be something like a friend.

"Nice juice box you got there, Pandora," a big burley inmate with cornrows smirked as she snatched the juice off of her tray and walked off.

"I didn't say you could have that," Pandora whispered to herself keeping her head down.

"What bitch? You got something to say? I don't see your funky ass body guard around here to fucking save your ass." The woman searched the chow hall looking for anyone who would help Pandora. "I didn't think so. Oh yeah, don't think I forgot you owe me that ass."

Everyday somebody new tried to pull it with Pandora. She was so tired of the shit, that she figured she would fight one of them just so they would kill her ass and free her from the torment. It was another reason why she stuck like glue to Oxy, but when her back was turned Pandora was free game. She lowered her head fighting back tears knowing she would never stand a chance against any of the big bitches that taunted her every day and decided it was time to get her backup secured. She took her tray tossing the contents in the trash and placed the tray on the lunch attendant's cart before heading to her cell to confront Oxy.

"Hey, what's your deal? All day you've been snotty with me and I ain't even done shit to you," Pandora voiced.

"Ugh, just go finish your damn lunch Pandora."

"No I will not go and finish shit until you tell me what the hell is wrong with you," Pandora pushed, increasingly becoming angry at the fact that Oxy was lying in the bed turned over facing the wall instead of her, "Will you please just fucking talk to me?"

"What do you want me to say? That you're making yourself look like a fucking ass every time you talk about being here, like it's going to make the situation any better. Or change the fact that I'm in love with you?" Oxy bellowed as she rose from the bottom bunk.

"Huh? In love with me," Pandora lowered her head into her hand wondering what brought this emotion on, "Oxy we barely know each other. I don't even like girls like that."

"Awww come on. You gon' sit here and tell me all that shit you told me you did with your lil' sister was bullshit. No sane person lies about that kind of shit," Oxy caressed the lower half of her cheek with the back of her hand.

It was at that moment that Pandora realized she had apparently done too much pillow talking with her. Her fling with Lexi was not something she was most proud of but it did happen and she could not for the life of her get those feelings out of her head. She missed Lexi's warm touch and soft skin tremendously but her betrayal and the fact that she teamed up with Diamond was unforgiveable. Pandora was uncertain if she knew how to be in a relationship with a female since Lexi was the dominant one and was the only woman she had ever been with.

"No, everything I told you was true. But I can't tell you that I love you, Oxy."

"You ain't gotta love me, that shit will come. Just tell me you will be my girl. That's it," Oxy could see the doubt in Pandora's eyes, "I can take care of you baby. I'll never let anything happen to you. All I ask is that you remain pure for me."

"Pure? I'm not a virgin anymore," Pandora laughed feeling silly to have to answer that question.

"No, pure as in don't fuck with nobody else. If you're my girl that shit belongs to me. The first time you give it away, it's tainted and so are you. Get me?" Oxy replied as a dark look formed on her face.

"Oh. Yeah, I get it. But why do you want me so bad? I'm not as perfect as you think I am."

"Pandora you're far from perfect. But so am I and that's the reason why we're perfect for each other. You're just as fucked up as I am but together we can be right."

"I don't know, Ox."

"Shit, what you don't know? We ain't got family. We all we got up in here. There's nobody out there checking for you or me in this bitch. Those motherfucka's out there living right, ya heard me? Good. So fuck what they think, this is about me and you boo," Oxy spat her game quickly.

"I just really don't know, Ox." Pandora shook nervously.

"Just tell me that I can lick that pretty little pussy one good time and if I don't blow your mind then you don't even have to answer my question.

After I finish, if all you can think about is me, then we are meant to be, bitch."

It was an offer Pandora knew she should have refused, but the throbbing in her pants told her otherwise. She knew that once she did this there was no going back and there was no backing down. Oxy would own her in the joint, but at least she would not have to worry about nobody fucking with her anymore. Oxy was a small little thing in size but she was 5'10" and could pack a punch like nobody's business. She needed that kind of manpower on her team if she was ever going to survive until her court date. Pandora looked deep into her eyes and knew that for whatever reason, Oxy was in love with her and that was a feeling she had not felt in a long time.

"Okay. You've got a deal. But only if you blow my mind Ox, otherwise no go." Pandora fingered her like she was a little child.

"Awe shit I ain't worried about that at all," Oxy smiled as she pulled Pandora in, tonguing her down sloppily.

"Ewe, what the fuck is you doing?"

"What's wrong?"

"What's wrong? You were all over me like a nasty, drooling dog in heat that's what's wrong.

Don't you know how to kiss?" Pandora asked quickly believing that Oxy was going to fail her own challenge.

"Yeah I know how to kiss girl. I was just a little excited you know. I ain't had any since I've been down and that's almost 83 days."

"Okay well I'm a little sex deprived as well, but damn, slow it down a notch," Pandora curled her upper lip like there was an awful smell in the room.

Oxy took the hint, realizing she may have been a little over anxious on her first approach as she moved in slower to get it right this time. She pecked Pandora's thick mouthwatering lips three times slowly leaving her eyes opened to catch her reaction to her subtle touch. Pandora's bottom lip quivered a bit as Oxy closed in, opening her mouth syncing it with hers, gently massaging their tongues together. No matter how much she tried, Pandora could not dominate her movements the way she wanted to. Oxy took control grabbing the back of her neck and pulling her waist in to brush softly up against hers.

"Oh shit, we better stop before somebody catches us in here. That shit ain't allowed and if they knew we were together they'd separate us quick," Oxy said backing up and checking the skinny rectangular shaped window embedded in their cell door, "Save that hot shit for tonight when the lights go out. I swear I'm gonna tear that shit up girl."

"Hmm, we'll see." Pandora snickered.

"Yeah we will see."

"Humph," Pandora sighed with a distressed look on her face.

"What? What's wrong now? Please tell me you ain't having second thoughts."

"Naw, naw nothing like that, I just realized that my little sister's birthday is tomorrow. She'll be seventeen."

"Humph." Oxy grimaced.

Chapter 2: "Cause you my little sister and I love you..." —Diamond

Lexi plopped down on the couch next to Diamond leaning her head on her shoulder. They were all still so relieved that they had come out of that whole ordeal unscathed and without consequence, that they have been discussing the details of that day for weeks. Crackling noises penetrated their ears as Kojack made coffee and cooked steak and scrambled eggs in the kitchen. The smell flowing into the room heightened their senses and elevated the rumble in their stomachs. Nothing was uttered as they sat quietly in the house even though everyone was surely thinking the exact same thing. They knew they were damn lucky to have gotten through that mess.

"Do you think we were bogus as hell for letting her go down by herself?" Lexi asked finally breaking the stillness, sounding as concerned as she possibly could.

"Naw, she's a big girl and can take care of herself. Besides, she would have dimed us out in a heartbeat," Diamond replied rubbing her hair gently.

"You think?"

"Lex, she tried to kill both of us and run off with all the damn money. That bitch didn't give two shits about us."

"Yeah, I know. It's just fucked up though. Whatever happened to the three musketeers?"

"What? Lex, have you been poppin' today? I sure ain't seen you pop them Yompers, but I know you keep a stash hidden somewhere. You're trippin', straight up."

"No Diamond I haven't popped in about two weeks. I'm thinking about quitting."

"Oh shit! Lil' sis got some good dick in her life and now she ready to turn her life over to Jesus. Hallelujah!" Diamond laughed hysterically.

"Naw, bitch I ain't say all that. I'm just saying I may slow down and quit that's all. Anyway, I just don't think Pandora is gonna last five seconds in jail." Lexi rolled her eyes at her sister's remark.

"Shit she should've thought about that. I mean, are you even listening to yourself? You are so concerned with her but she didn't give a damn about what was going to happen to you! She...wait!" Diamond raised her eyebrow eyeing Lexi, "Did you fuck her Lex?"

"Huh…uh…huh?"

"Bitch you heard what I said! Did you fuck her nasty ass?"

"No, Diamond no! Why would I do that? That's my sister yo, you crazy as hell."

"Awe bitch you did, didn't you? Awe Lex you can't be out here doing shit like that man. You bogus as hell! That's your damn sister, man. Y'all are fucking blood yo." Diamond covered her mouth with both of her hands in disgust. "All those times you tried to get me, I thought you was bullshitting girl, damn."

"Come on Diamond, you know me better than that. I wouldn't do any nasty shit like that."

"You're lying, Lex. I know you are."

"Is that something that she does often, lie?" Kojack interrupted with three cups of coffee in tow.

"No I don't lie often." Lexi snapped snootily.

"Then tell the truth. How did I find out that you two were sisters?" Kojack smirked taking a sip from his cup.

"Yeah Lex, you say you gonna stop poppin' Yompers and turn over a new leaf and shit. So start with telling the truth and not lying all the damn time." Diamond spat.

"Ugh, this shit is really starting to bring me down from the little happy high I did have." Lexi replied.

Silence fills the room. The only thing that could be heard around them was the sound of lips sipping from hot coffee mugs. Diamond and Kojack side eyed Lexi waiting to see if she was going to own up to her lies and finally come clean. They could tell by her demeanor of slouching down deep in the couch and her low eyes that she wasn't in the mood to change that instantly. Diamond had to admit that she already knew the answer to the question she had asked but it did not make her feel any better. As the older sister, Pandora should have known better even though it was apparent for years that she was not the brightest crayon in the box upstairs. Only after their dangerous encounter with Sun did Pandora open the evil, vindictive soul within her.

"Alright, you want me to start telling the truth? Then here's my fucking truth." Lexi said sitting up and placing her mug on the coffee table. "Yeah I fucked her, more than once too. She was damn good and her pussy tasted as sweet as honey. I tried to get you, but you were on some bullshit so I got the weakest one of the bunch. She liked that shit too and I'm almost pissed she's gone. I convinced thick dick over here into fucking me so we could get caught by her so we could both fuck her brains out, which was damn good too," Lexi answered.

"Oh my God, Lex—"

"Don't interrupt me. You wanted to hear it, right? So, after we fucked her I started wanting him because he was the only man that could make me cum like that and have my legs trembling. I couldn't quit fucking him, he was like my fix. I don't even need Yompers to fuck him that's how good he is. So as long as I got him I don't need shit else and that's part of the reason why I said I would quit poppin'." Lexi turned to her sister. "He's like my stress reliever, happy now?"

Kojack was so enamored and flattered by her confession that he could not even muster up a reply behind it. Diamond sat her cup on the table also impressed by her sister's affirmation and wanted to do one of her own. She knew that her truth would undoubtedly lead to dropped mouths and shocked eyes throughout the group but she figured it was as good a time as any to release her demon. She interlocked her fingers then placed her elbows on her knees looking around to see if anyone would say anything first.

"Lexi, I'm very proud of you for wanting to turn over a new leaf. I'm concerned that you are doing it for that reason but it is what it is. I'm also disappointed that you had to sleep with your sister in order to achieve that goal, but that is also some shit for another day." Diamond began.

"Well thanks, I guess."

"But since we are all airing out our dirty laundry I feel there are some things I want to get off my chest as well," Diamond continues, "So here it goes."

Diamond took a deep breath feeling the wind build up in her lungs as she closed her eyes and exhaled. She did not know how to deliver the information inside of her but she had a feeling her mouth would just naturally blurt it out like word vomit. She needed to get her mind together before it came out even though there was no time to do so. All eyes were on her as they waited patiently to see what she had to say. Diamond grabbed the hair in her ponytail twisting it around in her fingers searching for the right way to tell them her issues. A loud vibrating noise rattled the change in Kojack's cargo pants pocket as he dug deep into it pulling out his cell phone.

"Ay, hold that thought. I don't wanna miss this." Kojack said throwing his hand up for her to halt her announcement.

"Doesn't he have the sweetest little ass?" Lexi admired as her eyes followed while he gets up to leave the room.

"Lex, don't think you're off the hook for that nasty shit you did. I mean truly, that shit was foul. I could beat your ass for that, for real."

"Damn Diamond, learn to let shit go. It's obviously over between me and her and I'm never gonna see her again."

"Naw, I can't let it go, and actually I got a few motherfuckas on my list that got some shit coming from me too. I ain't never letting shit go from that," Diamond said curling her lips, "And I'm damn sure not through with Pandora's ass yet."

"Girl what the fuck you gonna do? She already suffering enough ain't she?"

"Naw, you don't know all the shit this bitch did to me."

"I'm listening."

"I'll tell you later."

"Damn you always do that Diamond. Why you be trying to save me from reality like I'm a little kid or somethin'? I can handle bad shit. Don't you know all the shit that I've done and been through?" Lexi snapped.

"If you think you can handle it, Lex," Diamond snapped, "Every time somebody tells you something you take it to heart and get to crying and shit."

"No I don't."

"Yes you do! You cry like a motherless child every time," Diamond paused realizing her onslaught of words might have been of poor choice, "Anyway, did you go to the doctor like I told you?"

"No, I haven't had time, D dang."

"Oh, but you've had time to spread your legs like an open book huh?"

"Damn, why you always trippin' on me?"

"Cause you my little sister and I love you. I'm not about to have you out here bogus and shit Lex. You gotta do better, you gots to. If not for me and if not for you then do it for momma. You know she wouldn't want us living this way," Diamond encouraged leaning her back against the couch focusing on the ceiling, "Damn I wish she was still here, man."

"Me too, maybe none of this shit would've ever happened to us," Lexi replied shaking her head.

"Ain't a maybe, I know none of this shit would have ever happened."

"Yeah."

Kojack slid sluggishly back into the room and sat down in his chair. He looked at the girls realizing they were in a heartfelt moment that he had missed. He didn't want to seem rude or inconsiderate of their feelings but he yearned to know what they talked about figuring Diamond had already spilled the beans. His cell went off again but he was determined to ignore it, pressing the silence button to shut it up. The job could wait a few minutes while he got the truth out in the open.

"So, what did I miss?" Kojack asked staring simultaneously at the girls for a response.

"Nothing, I was just telling Ms. Lexi here that her ass was grass once we get alone."

"Ugh." Lexi breathed rolling her eyes and slumping down in the couch.

"Alright then, spill it Diamond." Kojack said folding his hands eagerly.

"I'm not sure that this is the right time or place to have this discussion anymore. I mean, things are really crazy right now. We should be focusing on a plan to keep Pandora's ass in jail. You know, for her upcoming court date," Diamond said getting up from the couch and strolling over to the window.

"Keep her in jail? How she gonna get out?" Lexi inquired with a puzzled look on her face, "That bitch is dirty and it's going to be all over the nine o'clock news. She's fucked royally."

"Yeah but we need to get and keep our story together because we're going to need to testify. We need to work to make sure that the police and prosecutors have everything they need in order to convict that bitch of capital murder," Diamond replied looking out the window checking out the passing cars. "Even if that means we need to lay it on thick. We don't need that bitch twisting the story putting us in shit."

"D, the only way for us to do that, is if we implicate ourselves in that shit too. I'm not about to put myself nowhere near that scene or they gon' lock us up too," Lexi shook her head worriedly. "Bitch you crazy."

"Well maybe not. If you guys anonymously tip everything you know and maybe where they can find evidence then you should be okay. They may not need your testimony," Kojack interrupted, Google searching ways to report crimes on his phone.

"I'll testify." Diamond said softly.

"Excuse me, sis?"

"I said, I'll testify." Diamond was matter of fact.

"What? No, no you can't do that." Lexi freaked.

"Why not, someone has to be the witness right?"

"No Diamond! I've lost one sister; I refuse to lose another one."

"I'll just tell them that she told me about it when she came home. And when they ask me why I'm just now coming forward, I'll say because I was scared for my life."

"And if that doesn't work?" Kojack asked.

"Then I'll just take one for the team. But at least that bitch gets what she deserves."

"So you gonna sacrifice yourself for a vendetta? What about me, D? You're not even thinking about me. I can't lose another sister!" Lexi began to cry.

"See. I told you, you couldn't handle it," Diamond walked over and stroked her hair to console her, "Well dear sister, you might have to get used to one day living without me anyway."

"Huh?" Kojack raised his eyebrow.

"No never!" Lexi cried.

"Why Diamond?" Kojack asked curiously.

Diamond's palms filled with tiny droplets of sweat, afraid to tell them for fear of them treating her like a leper. Her heart could not bear that, as she looked deep into the eyes of the man she once craved and that of her seemingly naïve little sister. There were no words that would be able to prepare them for that kind of news. Her thoughts were as heavy as her heart as she looked deeply into her sister's inquisitive eyes and then cut away to the window, staring out into the white snow. For some reason she felt the truth would set her free right at that moment.

"Because I have AIDS lil' sis."

"Oh my God!" Lexi gasped. "Are you sure? How do you know?"

"I just know okay. Don't bombard me with fifty questions; just know that you need to be more careful lil sis. It can happen to anybody."

Kojack exhaled deeply, fixing his mouth like he was about to blow a whistle but only air came out. He sat back in his chair devastated by the news she had just dropped on them and it felt like a building of bricks. Lexi could do nothing more than hold her hand over her mouth to keep from giving Diamond the inquisition. The looks on both of their faces was more than she could bare as Diamond snatched her coat from the back of the dining room chair and headed for the door.

"Where are you going, Diamond? You just gonna leave like that?" Lexi asked feeling guilty that they might have been a little harsh in their reactions.

"I'm just going to get some air."

Chapter 3: "But it's my birthday." — Lexi

It was 4 pm. Lexi walked around Kojack's freshly cleaned house checking everything to make sure she had gotten dirt from every nook and cranny. She was becoming accustomed to being a little housewife and had virtually no complaints. It was everything she did not know she could be, but she knew that she wanted to keep Kojack happy. It was also her way of showing him that she and Diamond were appreciative of him letting them stay at his place until they got on their feet.

Lexi was not much of a cooker seeing as though Pandora used to handle all of that when they were living with their dad. But she was slowly coming into her own, learning to cook tacos, baked chicken, and fried cabbage, which were recipes she looked up on YouTube. Today was a special day, though. She sought out a bunch of recipes fit for a king and decided to whip them up like nobody's business. Kojack would be home from work at 6 pm and she wanted to make sure that dinner was piping hot and on the table by 5:55 pm and not a moment later.

All of the burners on the stove were lit high and the oven, along with the steam from the pots made the kitchen feel like a sweltering jungle. She smiled to herself realizing her meal was almost complete, baked macaroni and cheese, cornbread muffins, baked barbequed ribs, corn on the cob, and Glory greens. Even though she had not seen Diamond all day she made enough for her to eat as well. It was weird to her how Diamond was always up and out of the house by the time she woke up in the morning, but she brushed it off figuring she was out looking for them an apartment with the money they stole from Pandora. Lexi did not know a good way to tell Diamond that she was not going to move with her feeling like Kojack needed her more. The longer she could postpone the talk the better.

"Hey babe, I was just calling to see how much longer it will be before you get home," Lexi exclaimed when Kojack answered the phone.

"Uh, I got at least a few more hours here. Some shipments didn't come in today and we have to do a few things with what we got here so…it's a bit rough right now," Kojack's voice was dry and uninviting.

"Okay, I'm sensing some issues on your end. You having a rough day at work and need someone to talk to or what?"

"Naw Lex. I'm just working right now, okay. When I'm done I'll be home."

"Kojack…it's 5:30 pm though. I mean, how long do you think you're gonna be?"

"If I knew I'd tell you but right now, I don't know."

"Okay listen, I feel the hostility flowing through the phone. I ain't done anything wrong so I'm trying to figure out why I'm being punished. I should be happy today babe, but for some reason I don't feel happy," Lexi whined.

"Look we can talk about this later alright. I gotta go."

"Kojack, why can't we fucking talk about it now? You obviously have some issues that you need to air out so why not do it now so when you get home everything will be good. Cause all I'm trying to do tonight is eat good and damn sure fuck good."

"Bye Lex. I'll be home when I'm done," Kojack was stern as he hung up the phone.

"Kojack! Kojack!" Lexi looked at the phone in disbelief that he had hung up on her when she clearly was not done talking.

She knew that he was a little uneasy after Diamond's confession of her illness yesterday but what she did not know is how badly it had affected him. Lexi was not about to let it mess her day up, though. It was her birthday and she was seventeen now, which meant she was one year closer to being a full grown woman. She was one year closer to Kojack not having to worry about what people thought of their relationship and gossiping about her age. As she removed the homemade cake from the stove that she poured blood, sweat and tears into, because Kojack was nuts about homemade sweets, she was determined not to allow his funky demeanor on the phone to deter her from thinking about celebrating tonight.

All of the burners and oven were off and the cake was frosted with caramel. She made sure to cover the food properly so that it retained its heat. The time seemed to escape her but she knew that no matter how late he said he had to work, Kojack would never let her down knowing that today was very special for the two of them. She whisked up the stairs and into the shower for the second time that day, posthaste. He liked a fresh kitty cat to nibble on and wanted to make sure she served him just that. Once she was done, she decided to let her bobbed hair air dry to give it a curly look. The heat was so intense in the house that the droplets of water on her body nearly evaporated immediately.

Lexi had never gone back to their downtown condo ever since the day Pandora was arrested, so she had virtually no clothes at Kojack's house and Diamond seemed to be hoarding the money tightly. Nonetheless, she figured what better way to ring in her birthday than nearly in her birthday suit, adorning only a pair of lace black thongs she had on hand. She waltzes back down the stairs swaying her hips and bouncing her breasts practicing how she would greet him when he came through the door. She twirled around in circles enjoying how free she felt as the air caressed her curvy body. She glanced over at the cable box to peep the time, 6:58 pm.

To occupy her time she went to set the dining room table with a romantic setting. Lexi grabbed two China plates from the cabinet of dishes that were on display in the dining room. Kojack obviously only used those for exhibition purposes, but tonight was so extraordinary that she knew he would not care. She removed two sparkling glasses from the cabinet as well and placed them neatly in front of the plates. Unfortunately Kojack did not have any expensive silverware so she just folded some paper towels for napkins and used the standard forks and knives from the kitchen drawer to complete the table setting.

When the table was perfectly set to her liking, Lexi sauntered over to the stereo in the corner behind the sofa, pressing the power button before turning the volume up loudly.

At last

My love has come along

My lonely days are over

And life is like a song

Oh yeah yeah

At last

The skies above are blue

My heart was wrapped up in clover

The night I looked at you

Etta James seemed to be speaking straight to Lexi's soul as if she had written the song specifically for her and Kojack. She danced like a stunning ballerina around the living room miming the words as if she were Etta herself, performing her own little concert with her eyes closed. Once the song was over, the radio DJ spoke about various concerts in the area toning down for his commercial break while an out of breath Lexi plopped down on the sofa. The clock read 7:50 pm as her patience slowly began to wear thin from waiting to celebrate another year of life with the one she loved. She moved towards the kitchen popping the chilled Chardonnay she had on ice for the both of them to enjoy. It was the only thing of substance that she had to calm her nerves.

Meanwhile, Kojack sat in front of his house staring at the light shining through his living room curtains. He looked over in the passenger seat at the small neatly wrapped gift box with a curly shimmering gold bow on top of it. The wrapping paper was red with gold celebration dots. Lexi loved the color gold but that was the only paper they had left to wrap the two carat diamond tennis bracelet that he had bought for her. He purposely did not wish her a happy birthday all day because he was waiting to whisper it in her ear after she had opened her gift. But for some reason his legs could not move out of the car, his arms could not grasp the handle and pull the door open, and his fingers could not allow him to turn the key to the ignition shutting the car off.

He knew she would be in there; waiting for him in some sexy lingerie hoping for him to pummel her ass something wicked. He licked his lips at the very thought of her sweet juices. But even though he yearned to touch her, hold her, something deep down inside of him held him back from the act. The lump in his throat did not seem to go away no matter how many times he swallowed but he took a deep breath and closed his eyes picturing the train wreck ahead. He exited the car slowly and quietly looking around at the near darkness of the street. The cold air slapped him in the cheeks and the brisk tickled his nose as he sniffed hard to keep the snot from leaving his nose in a drip.

"Ahhh!" Kojack exhaled as he muscled up the courage to head towards the house and walk up his own flight of stairs to the front door.

He took out his house keys fiddling with them for a few minutes before setting the box down on the step in front of the glass screen door. His eyes stared down at it as if it would magically unlock the door and walk into the house on its own. It was a bitch move, a cowardly move and he knew it but was too afraid to fight it. It felt as if there was not a chance in hell that he would survive the night with her knowing what he knew. As painful as it was for him, he raced down the stairs and jumped back into his car. His legs shook but not from the cold as he revved up the engine. He took one last look at his house, feeling nothing but guilt mixed with a smidgen of relief as the car slowly rolled away from the house.

"Kojack?" Lexi called out coming from the kitchen to the living room.

She thought she had heard a noise and

hoped it was him coming in the door. On her third glass of wine and trying not to guzzle it like she did the first two, she sauntered over to the dining table with the Chardonnay bottle in tow. She placed it down in front of her plate and stared into the flowered centerpiece as she sipped from her glass. With every sip she could feel her soul crush into many pieces. Never before had she loved someone so deep and cared about someone so much, not even Pandora. She grabbed her cell and dialed his number already knowing he would not answer the phone. He proved her right. She tossed it out of her sight hearing it land on the coffee table behind her and thankful that it did not shatter. After that scare, the thought of wrecking something entered her brain but she feared it might be premature since he could walk through that door at any given minute.

'*Just calm down Lex he'll be here. He loves you,*' Lexi recited to herself over and over again as the tears fell one by one allowing her eyes to glance over at the time, 9:15 pm.

She stood walking over to the window hoping to see his car parked out front with him in it or see him just pulling up but it was to no avail. Her eyes drifted over to her left noticing that the screen door was slightly open. It was never open like that, leaving her with a bit of suspicion in the back of her head, enough to make her go check it out. The cold air brushed against her half naked skin roughly, sending chills and shivers throughout as she tiptoes her bare feet into the short small hallway, opening the wooden door. Graced at her feet was a tiny shiny box with a beautiful neatly tied bow on top. As she picked it up it was then and only then that reality kicked in informing her that no matter how optimistic she was about their relationship, one thing was clear, he was not.

'But it's my birthday,' she whimpered.

*****

"Damn, Ox. We ain't gotta fuck every night. You proved your point last night and now I'm yours but cool it tonight. Will you?" Pandora turned over punching her pillow before dumping her head down on it.

"Now we was good all day and all of a sudden you trippin'. You need me to munch on that thang to put you in a good mood or what?" Ox said running her hand inside of her pants, massaging her ass cheeks.

"I just don't wanna fuck tonight. Is that cool with you?"

Pandora's words cut through Ox like a box cutter as she abruptly exited her bunk returning to the top. She crossed her arms balling up into a tight ball with a shitty look on her face. It was weird for her to feel emotionally abandoned knowing that Pandora did not love her the way she did, but her feelings were strong and she could not fake them.

"You mad now?" Pandora asked feeling like she may have been a little wrong.

"It's her isn't it?"

"Ugh," Pandora sighed, "She's my sister, Ox and it is her birthday. I'm just thinking about her, that's all."

"That bitch doesn't care about you, not the way I do."

"I know that, Ox. It's just—"

"Pandora, either you love her or you fuck with me. It's your choice. But I refuse to live in the shadow of some young broad you ain't supposed to be fucking with in the first place."

"Excuse me?"

"You heard me. Choose. It's me or her."

"Why you gotta make it like that? She's always going to be my sister and nothing's going to change that. So your ultimatum is pointless."

Pandora rose from her bed smiling at Ox's jealousy. It was cute, the way she was protective of her feelings, cute yet scary. She climbed into the bed gently tickling Ox's legs with her fingertips along the way before connecting, spooning with her. Their bodies fused together effortlessly as if they were meant to fit together, like they were the two missing pieces to a puzzle. For the first time since she met Pandora, Ox felt like she was hers and no one else's. She feels like Pandora knows who she is and could sense why she loves her so. They were reading each other's minds without even uttering a word and yet so much was spoken. It was the first time that Ox was that close to a woman and was not even thinking about planting her waist on her face.

"I do love her but you are my bitch and that's all that matters. I only think of her when I think of how those bitches fucked me over. I just want what they have," Pandora spoke sweetly, stroking her hair.

"Oh yeah, what's that?" Ox mumbled.

"Freedom," Pandora paused allowing time for the message to sink in, "Ox, you gotta help me baby."

"Help you do what?" Ox inquired in a dry manner.

"Help me escape. I can't rot away in this jail cell knowing these motherfuckas are out there living the good life," Pandora whispered casually licking the back of her left ear, "I deserve better."

"I know you do boo," Ox replied patting her hand softly.

"So how we gon' get out of here?"

"Pandora, I ain't got a way of getting out of here. That's crazy talk."

"We got to figure something out, you know. We can't get married in jail."

"Wait, what?"

"You heard me. I think you're the bitch for me, Ox. But I can't marry you in this hell hole."

"Oh my God Pandora, you just made me the happiest bitch in the world!"

"Shh! Calm down before they hear us. Don't go getting all excited and we ain't even free yet."

"Okay, okay. I'm gonna think of something. I don't know what yet, but you best believe that

I'm gon' think of something," Ox turned over squeezing her ass as tight as could be, never wanting to release it.

"You do that," Pandora grinned slyly.

Chapter 4: "Like I said bring it on bitch!"– Diamond

The next morning Lexi awoke in Kojack's bed cold and alone. The sheets grazed her naked body as she sat up looking around the room hoping to find signs of his presence. When there was none, she grabbed his old large white t-shirt off the floor and stood sliding it over her head letting it drape to her knees. Once covered, she heads out of the room to search the house for signs of life but found only silence. It pained her, feeling empty inside thinking that Kojack had slipped in last night and out this morning without a trace. She picks up her cell from off the coffee table, and then fumbled through it discovering not one missed call. Her head hung low, she slew footed into the kitchen to snag some breakfast and was startled, jumping back by Diamond's face.

"Damn girl! Why are you sitting in here quiet and shit? I thought everyone was gone," Lexi said reaching for a bowl out of the cabinet as she tries to erase the disappointment that had fallen on her face.

"I couldn't sleep. I know I won't have much time on this earth so I need to get some affairs in order before I leave," Diamond spat as she took a bite of the toast on her plate then sat it back down next to the eggs, rubbing her fingers together relieving them of excess crumbs.

"Ugh!" Lexi groans slamming the box of Apple Jacks down on the counter, "I wish you would quit talking like that. I've only known of your condition for twenty four hours and already I want to cry every minute for you. You saying shit like this ain't gonna help me."

"It's the truth, Lex. The sooner you come to that realization the better off we'll both be."

"But D, there's plenty of medications out there that can help you and the baby live a long and healthy life."

"Baby? Bitch I'm not raising no damn babies. This little shit is going to die in my body with me because I ain't taking any meds, nothing. I just want to die happy knowing I've sought revenge on the motherfuckas who deserves it," Diamond snapped angrily.

"You sound like a fucking demon, yo. I can't believe you are that thoughtless. That life growing inside of you is a blessing and didn't ask to be made. You could at least give it a chance at life."

"For what, I can't take care of it. I'm gonna be dead anyway so what's the point. I don't want it growing up knowing that I did this to it. So I'd rather just end its life before it starts. Besides, revenge is the only thing I care about right now," Diamond headed over to the trash to throw the rest of her breakfast away.

"Ugh. Revenge this and revenge that. What is that even going to solve?" Lexi bellowed as she sat down at the table.

"It's going to help me die happy knowing motherfuckas will be dancing in hell with me," Diamond laughed swaying her hips erotically from left to right.

Lexi fiddled her spoon around in her bowl of cereal realizing she had not even put the milk in it as yet. The more she looked at it the more she felt as though her hunger pangs had diminished from Diamond's inconsiderate words. Her conversation with Diamond was pissing her off beyond measure making it impossible to focus on or think about anything else. She flicked her bob cut and prayed that the knowledge she was about to release from her mouth would bring her sister back down to reality.

"Diamond, you are grown and I can't tell you what to do. But if you think that killing off the people who wronged you will make you happy, you're crazy. You need to focus on the life inside you and give yourself a chance as well. You are too young for this shit."

"Okay you know what? I'm gonna need for you to drop this shit. I'm not going to change my mind and I'm going to do what I want to do. So you either get over it or you leave me the fuck alone. You're my lil' sis and I love you but don't get on my bad side, alright?" Diamond walked off heading to the living room.

"Well what about the baby, Diamond?" Lexi roared following right behind her.

"What about it?"

"Give it to me." Lexi spewed tears from her eyes as she gazed upon the confused look on her sister's face, "Give it to me and I'll take care of it. Just um, take the meds for as long as you're pregnant and then when you give birth, give it to me. Please!"

Diamond exhaled lowering her head then raised it smiling back at her, "Why do you want this so badly?"

"Because you keep saying that you're gonna die, if that's true, I at least want a piece of you still around. I've lost one sister; at least I can have a part of the other one."

The tears flowed like a faucet from Lexi's eyes. She did not know what made Diamond so coldhearted but she felt that giving up on her would be giving up on her, would be niece or nephew. There was a life so innocent and so pure growing inside of her and she had no emotional ties to it whatsoever. Staring at Lexi's tears made her feel remorse, briefly.

"The baby didn't ask to be made, Diamond. Please just think of someone harmless. Think of someone other than yourself," Lexi pleaded.

"Okay! Sheesh, don't lose your mind. I'll think about it. Think! Do you understand?" Diamond retorted sternly pointing her finger.

"That's all I could ask for right now. Now where are you going?" Lexi asked as she watched Diamond slip on her coat.

"I need to go do some research about something. I'll be back later."

"Diamond," Lexi side eyed.

"Don't worry, don't worry. I'll be back," She laughed as she heads out of the front door.

"You missed my damn birthday!" Lexi bellowed trying to get a word in edgewise before Diamond stumbles out the door.

Diamond retraced her steps back inside shutting the door behind her in total dismay. She could not believe that she was so caught up in her own stalking affairs that she forgot her favorite sister's birthday. She saw the pain and hurt in Lexi's eyes and knows that her hurt runs deeper than just her forgetfulness. There was an underlying problem there and judging by the food that was left out on the stove and the well-designed layout on the dining room table that was left untouched, it had something to do with Kojack.

"Baby sis, I am so sorry about yesterday. I hate to say I totally forgot but…"

"It doesn't matter. I mean you've got your own thing going on and I respect that and Kojack has work. It's cool. It's cool," Lexi interrupted while she allowed the tears to continue down her chubby cheeks.

"No it is not ok. We are going to go out and we are going to do whatever it is you want to do! Come on, get dressed," Diamond sat beside her stroking tears from off her cheeks as they fell.

"D, I don't feel like doing shit now. I just wanna lay here and wither away."

"Up, now, bitch! I ain't got time for you feeling sorry for yourself now. You're better than that. Fuck that nigga. If he can't see how special you are then fuck him."

"Don't talk bad about him, Diamond. He probably just got caught up at work."

"Hmm. Yeah whatever, just get dressed," Diamond said checking her cell for the first time, "I just gotta make one stop first and by the time I get back you should be ready right?"

"Yeah I guess so," Lexi shook her head thinking bullshit just flew from Diamond's mouth. She knew they were not going to celebrate and did not even bother to oblige her request to get dressed.

Diamond jetted out the door quickly and walked over to her car then hopped in. Driving down the road all she could think about was what she would do when she got to her destination. Her adrenaline was pumping through her veins like gas at a station and it felt damn good. Twenty minutes later she pulled up in front of the house next door to Tino's. She sat there as if she was on a stakeout waiting for something to happen, waiting for the moment to present itself on the outside of the house. For the last week, she had been watching Tino's every move making sure she had him down to a science. It was important for her to study him so she would not be caught slipping once she moved in for the kill.

Just as the sun crept across the snow shining brightly on the house, she noticed there was minimal movement at the front door. A female exited the house and walked around to the back carrying a small plastic bag full of trash. Right after her, Tino and a man exited the house standing on the stoop together. His very existence made her skin crawl. Her breathing increased as her eyebrows frowned. She wanted to hop out the car and slit both of their throats much like Pandora had done to Sun, a clean sweep from ear to ear. Diamond tried to envision what it would be like to watch his blood squirt out of his neck and stand over him as he struggled to breathe. She wanted his gurgling to manifest in his brain so that it was the last thing he heard before his heart stopped and his soul drifted off to his rightful home, hell.

"Ugh!" she growled lightly as she watched them make out heavily on his door stoop, "Nasty motherfucka, so that's how you got AIDS...fucking other niggas with no condoms."

Diamond popped her knuckles, one right after the other, licking her lips simultaneously as if she was about to pounce and maul her prey. She quickly ran ideas through her head as to how she would make him suffer. Once the light bulb went off, she knew what tools she needed to get the job done. The anticipation grew with every waning second fucking with her mental, desiring his blood sooner than later. She waited for the love fest to end as the chick returned from behind the house, walking up to them and joining them in their tongue lashing. It sickened Diamond even more to watch, turning her head until the man walked off. The clock on the dash read 9:30 am on the dot as the man headed towards his car and his playmates headed back into the house.

"You sorry piece of shit, dying of AIDS is too good for you. Naw, you've gotta pay for what you've done, for all the lives you've ruined. Give me a few days and I got you motherfucka," Diamond snarled as she started her car and drove off finding herself unconsciously following the man in the car.

The man seemed to be swerving as if he were drunk or high. It was dangerous for her to follow him especially with the slush and sleet on the road but something inside of her needed to see his face. Diamond pressed her foot on the gas to speed up before the other cars got in the way. It was morning rush hour traffic, which made it difficult to keep up with anyone. The man appeared to have sped up his car and as he bobbed and weaved in and out of lanes, he nearly nicked a car trying to run a red light. He made it but she did not, having been stopped by the Ford truck in front of her, infuriating Diamond to no end.

"Dammit!" she snapped banging her fist on the steering wheel profusely in a wail of a tantrum.

As she sat there she realized how foolish she was to follow him when her beef was not even with that man. It had become apparent that after a week of stalking Tino and learning his everyday habits and rotation, she had become not only obsessive but also insane. She could think, eat, or drink of nothing else but her revenge on this man. The light turned green and as she merged on to the expressway she knew that it was time to eliminate her obsession before it destroyed her. It was one thing to consume her life but it would not kill her, at least not before she had the chance to kill him first. She was no clown though.

Bringing nothing to a gunfight would surely get her planted six feet deep with nothing to show for it. This was a game she was going to play well but not fair in order to win and knew she needed some heavy firepower to get the job done. En route, her cell buzzed like crazy in her pocket and as bad as she did not want to answer it, she did it only because she knew who it was.

"Yeah Lex."

"It's not Lex, bitch."

"Pandora…if it isn't my selfish, evil, bitch of a twin, how are you toots? Jailed, I hope," Diamond's voice sounded smug.

"You would like that wouldn't you? That was a bitch move you pulled and you know it. You know just as well as I do that you belong in that fucking jail cell right along with me!" Pandora bellowed. "That shit was all your idea."

"Yeah, but it wasn't my idea to cut him open like a Christmas ham now was it? No bitch that was all you."

"Well somebody had to stand up and take control of the situation. Your weak ass didn't."

"Ugh, what the fuck do you want, Pandora?"

"Oh, right. I almost forgot. I just called to tell you that I love you big sis. But your ass is going down. You and that slut of a sister of yours are dead."

"Don't speak love to me hoe, when you damn sure don't know the meaning of it and as for your idle threats, I'm shaking in my boots, P."

"You should be. See you would've been dead but I guess if you want shit done you've gotta do it yourself," Pandora sucked her teeth. "And I want my fucking money back. I know you and that slut stole me shit."

"What money? Awe sis, you know me better than that," Diamond grinned.

"You're right. I do know you better than that, we're twins, remember? I know you are the only one who could pull off taking my shit without a fucking trace. So here's how it's gonna go down. You give me my fucking money and I just might think about letting you two bitches live," Pandora smirked.

"I don't know what the hell you're talking about and you scare no one bitch. Bring it on. Oh and Lex told me to tell you that Kojack's dick tasted mighty good last night. A taste, you'll surely miss," Diamond laughed as she hung up the phone.

The phone immediately rang back. It rang again and again until Diamond reluctantly answered, "What!"

"When you die, I'm going to take pleasure in watching you beg for your life. I'm going to cut off every limb you have including your tits and watch you bleed to death while you beg for mercy, bitch."

"My tits, ewe, sounds like sexual

harassment if you ask me. I mean, Lex told me she banged you but I never thought she would be able to turn you into a dike!" Diamond guffawed wildly.

"Argh! Shut up, shut up! You and that little bitch are fucking dead!" Pandora screamed in a low voice through the phone.

"Meanwhile, don't they record these phone calls in jail? They really gonna keep your ass now. Watch out for those spoons!"

"Who said I was using a jail phone? Watch your back, ho."

"Like I said, bring it on bitch," Diamond recited to herself as she pushed the END button and placed the phone back inside her pocket.

Chapter 5: "Not until you're eighteen." — *Kojack*

Kojack moved through the crowd tapping his hard hat making sure it was on securely. It was lunchtime and his face adorned the same look all day, distress. The thoughts in his head plagued him all day no matter how hard he worked to get his mind off of the situation. He talked with his workers and buried his self in blueprints but it seemed like the more he worked the more the thoughts flooded his brain.

"Hey guys I'm out for the day," Kojack hollered to his main manager as he waved them off and headed back to the car.

He sighed deeply as he sat in his car staring at his phone struggling with whether or not he should make a phone call. His heart was beyond heavy as he tried to calm his nerves. One touch of the number in his call log sent the call as he placed the phone up to his ear waiting for an answer.

"Hey baby," Lex answered enthusiastically.

"Uh, hey," Kojack breathed as he started up the car.

"Okay, so I was thinking we would go out

for dinner tonight, just you and me. What do you say?"

"Lex..."

"Because I was thinking like I could cook something but you don't really have any food in there and I'm not really a good cook so it's a no brainer," Lexi giggled as she rambled on.

"Listen, listen, we need to talk."

"If this is about this morning, I'm so sorry I overslept. I wanted to be there for you before you went to work but you didn't wake me up. Shit after waiting up so late for you last night baby, I was dog tired," Lex snickered playfully.

"No, no it's not that. I didn't even come home last night, Lex. You didn't notice?"

"Oh God," Lexi said gripping her stomach feeling as though it was jumping through hoops, knowing the storm that was coming.

Apart of her knew that the unspoken elephant in the room was eventually going to mutter its first words. It was the inevitable but she had hoped that it was something that would work itself out without complication. Her forehead became riddled with sweat bullets as she took a seat at the dining room table, breaking from the cleaning she was doing.

"Yeah, you have to understand Lex that I truly do love what we're doing here but we can't go on like this. I'm risking my reputation, my business, and my freedom fucking with you."

"Jack we've been through this…"

"I'm just afraid of losing everything that I worked so hard for over some pussy."

"Well, what if I said I wanted to be more than just pussy to you?" Lex sounded like she was about to break down in tears.

Even though she put on the facade like she could never love anyone, she could not help the feelings she felt for him. He was something real in her world full of mystery. He was the calm in her world full of chaos and destruction. She knew if she lost that goodness that her world would go tumbling back down again. Her age was the only deciding factor in their relationship and though it was a major factor she could not allow it to be the only one.

Lexi slapped her hands against her forehead multiple times before it gives her a headache. She was fucked up in the head by Kojack's cold words. It sounded as if he did not care about her. Her heart cracked into a million pieces wondering if he had ever allowed himself to feel anything for her. The age difference was the one hurdle she did not know how to get over. All she could do is replay the moment he found out and the person who spoke the thought into his mind.

"That bitch!" she screamed as she wiped tears from her already drenched cheeks and swung her arms knocking the flower vase off of the table.

It felt good to hit something. She lifted the dining room table tipping it over letting the loud crash sound that it made soothe her some more. Her eyes cased the living room for more things she could destroy before they zeroed in on the bright yellow sunlight shining through the kitchen window. Kojack heard the crashing of things in the background and automatically knew she was destroying his house. He lowered his head deciding not to confront her about it feeling like if that was what she needed to vent then so be it.

"Lex, there's no way I can have a relationship with you. Not until you're eighteen."

"But I just turned seventeen yesterday, that's almost eighteen and might I add that you didn't even think enough of me to come home or call or shit to wish me a happy one. But I'm willing to look past all of that and assure you that no one will ever know. I'll...I'll dress older and only go out where people won't notice how young I am."

"Lex…"

"I'll act very adult and make sure that I don't act immature and shit around your family and friends."

"Lex!"

"Kojack, please!" Lexi sobbed, "Please don't do this to us. We need each other. I need you. You're the only thing that keeps me clean."

"See girl. That's insanity. You think just because I eat pussy really good that you don't need Yompers but you never needed or wanted them in the first place. You're too young for me but you're old enough to realize that what we're doing is wrong."

"Kojack, I am begging you. Do not do this to us."

"Lexi, you and Diamond can live at my house for a few weeks until you guys find someplace to stay. I can find somewhere to go for a while."

"Kojack! Kojack, wait!"

"You'd better go get tested, Lexi."

He had hung up the phone as her cries

blurted through his receiver. He tossed the phone in the passenger seat as it rang and vibrated profusely hopping around. He ignored it turning the volume up on the radio to drown out its excessive badgering. As he drove on, he tried to put Lexi out of his mind for good. It was usually easy for him to write people out of his life for the sake of protecting his own feelings but the fact that his emotions were deeply involved with her made it difficult.

Kojack knew it would not be easy but he had to forget her. He had to block the erotic nights and sensational mornings out of his mind. He needed to get her sweet watermelon smell out of his head and her angelic touch off of his skin. Lexi had made her mark on him like a dog marked a tree. She was his and he knew it but the smart thing to do was the right thing to do. Kojack pulled up in the Northwestern Memorial Hospital parking garage. As he pulled his ticket out of the machine and drove under the raised partition, he began to fear knowing the results of the test he had taken this morning. Truth was, he was far past scared of even taking the test but he had to know. As he exited his Lexus truck headed for the elevator, he felt lumps of coal develop in his heart. He could not decipher if it was love or lust for her that he felt, he just wanted whatever it was to go away so the hurt would not bleed out of his veins.

****

"What the fuck just happened in here? I was only gone for a minute," Diamond asked stepping over the debris of Lexi's storm with her black suitcase in hand.

She walked up to a balling, wet faced Lexi sitting in front of the sofa on the floor and sat down stroking her hair gently for comfort. The whole house was a mess, riddled with broken glass and apparently a broken heart. Much like Lexi, Diamond knew it was only a matter of time before the shit hit the fan. Kojack was obviously more man than she could handle anyway. It was just sad that everyone knew it but her.

"You were gone for four hours Diamond. You're so full of shit," Lexi sobbed as she shook her head at her sister's previous lie.

"Okay but what's wrong, Lex?" Diamond inquired worried that a burglar might have come in and raped her.

"He broke up with me," Lexi stumbled through her cries. "I never knew I could be in love with somebody like that until I met him."

"Awe baby, you can't break up with someone you were never with," The words flew from Diamond's mouth without haste and once they did she instantly felt that they came out the wrong way.

"Huh?" Lexi used the back of her hand to wipe the drippings from her nose, "If this is your fucking way of cheering me up then you are failing, miserably."

"Lex, all I'm trying to get you to understand is that you both knew what this was, sex. So for you to try and make this arrangement more is crazy, especially when you both knew you weren't supposed to be fucking in the first place."

"I just thought he would be the one person to look past all that shit, D."

"He can't look past it because if he does he risks going to jail for you. This is Illinois baby. They ain't playing that shit here. Your homey, lover friend will get locked up in a heartbeat."

"But I want him. We are soul mates. We're meant to fucking be!" Lexi yelled as she banged on the coffee table hoping to break it.

"Stop!" Diamond shouted grabbing her sister's arms and holding them close, "Honey, you are so young and beautiful. You can have any man out here or woman for that matter; just choose someone your age."

"But I don't want anyone my age. I want him, Diamond, just him."

Diamond knew that no matter what she said to try and break her thoughts of being with him, Lexi was adamant on loving only him. Having been there and done that before, she knew exactly what her young sister was going through. She realized that stubbornness was a trait that ran in their family. They were relentless women who never stopped until they got what they wanted. Checking the room for its disaster once more, she felt it was best she just changed the subject.

"Pandora called me this morning," Diamond said wiping the tears from her sister's eyes.

"What? She's out of jail?"

"I don't know. She claimed she wasn't using a jail phone so I'm thinking that someone probably posted bail for the bitch."

"Well…what did she say?"

"She knows about the money…" Diamond sighed leaning back on the sofa, locking her eyes with the ceiling, "And she threatened us. She said she wants to kill us. I think she thinks that will keep us from testifying against her. Either way, I know she wants revenge."

"Ugh, now this shit. What the fuck are we gonna do? We ain't got fucking heat and I know that bitch gon' cop her something. She ain't gon' bring just a knife to fight," Lexi stood walking around in circles.

"Calm down. That bitch ain't gon' make her presence known til she's ready. The fact that she called let me know that she's looking for a battle. That bitch thinks she's an army or something. So we got the money to do what we need to do."

"That's still not telling me shit, D., and how the fuck did she find out that we stole the money? It could've been anybody."

"She thinks she knows we did it but I gave her no info. I guess she thinks we're the only ones capable of doing it. We're just gonna gear up and be ready for that bitch, simple as that," Diamond smirked, "If we go down, we damn sure will do it swinging."

"Man, I ain't got time to be going to war with this bitch," Lexi replied picking up broken pieces of glass to throw in the trash.

"Huh? Awe, come on now. Shit, I'm glad

this nigga broke up with you. He's makin' you soft as hell. Girl you need to get up out of that shit."

"What the fuck you mean, Diamond? This shit was always between you and Pandora. I was never in that shit; y'all just put me in it."

"Alexis Burden, you were in it the minute you decided to keep Kojack for yourself. Don't you see, kitten. He's the root to all evil," Diamond said shaking her head in disbelief at how naïve Lexi really was.

"No. No I won't believe that. Pandora's just a crazy bitch who needs to be stopped."

"And none of us had any problems until he came into the picture. We were a team."

"Diamond you need to get it together. Pandora never cared shit about us after that night. The night she tasted blood for the first time, you said it yourself. It's all about money; it was always just about the money," Lexi grabbed the broom and began sweeping up the broken pieces of her relationship, "Get a clue."

"Ugh, whatever bitch, just take that fucking suitcase and put it under the kitchen sink for me, would ya?" Diamond snapped as she headed for the staircase beginning to mumble. "And shut the fuck up. Damn."

Diamond ran upstairs heated from their discussion while Lexi did what was asked of her. No matter how naïve Lexi seemed, she sure had a way with words. She headed into Kojack's room looking at the unkempt king sized waterbed in the middle of the room thinking about all the wild nights they could have had. As quickly as those thoughts ran through her head, soon did ones of despair from the reality of the life threatening disease that she could not get rid of. With that thought she began to think of everyone else she could have passed it to as well. It only fueled the anger inside of her more to want to get rid of the problem once and for all so that he could not destroy any more lives with his infection.

She went over to his dresser where he held a collection of cologne and grooming products. Her eyes gleamed with admiration; it was nice to know that he was indeed the well-groomed stud she had always believed he was. Turning away, a shiny reflection distracted her, stopping her in her tracks. Something in hiding was using the sun to make a shiny reflection. It was very small but with the sun's rays it shone brightly. She kneeled down and reached her hand behind the dresser where the shine was coming from and pulled out a clean silver Revolver. It was small but a gun nonetheless. Diamond felt like she hit the jackpot, just in case she was unable to get one before Pandora caught up with them. She quickly stuffed it in the back of her jeans and left the room sight unseen.

Chapter 6: "I meant it when I told you I could give you anything." — Oxy

"I spoke to my dad today." Oxy said taking a sip from her juice carton.

"Yeah, yeah, he calls to check up on you blah, blah. What are you telling me that for?" Pandora snapped back ripping a small peel from her orange.

"Yeah," Oxy sighed bowing her head. "But what I never told you is his name."

"Huh? What the fuck does his name have to do with anything? You know, I'm getting tired of this shit Ox. If you can't deliver just say you can't instead of stringing me along."

Pandora stormed off dumping her tray before heading to the second tier to their cell. She wanted to cry, being mad at herself that her plan was not working but before she could muscle out a single tear, Oxy came bursting into the cell faster than a speeding bullet. The look on her face could have burned a whole through a thick brick wall as she stared down upon Pandora's head. She knew it had been a couple of days since she told her she would help her get out but it took her that much time to muscle up the courage to use her only sure fire resource.

"Before you storm off and lose your mind you need to learn to listen. I wasn't done yet," Oxy blurted lifting her head up, grabbing her cheeks and squeezing them together forcefully.

Pandora batted her hands away angrily. "What is it that I need to listen to? You obviously don't wanna marry me, because if you did we wouldn't be here. You're not trying hard enough, Ox!"

"Will you shut the fuck up and just listen?"

"Alright," Pandora exhaled. "I'm listening."

"My dad's name is Ivan Smear, the State's Attorney," Oxy replied lowering her head.

The shock in her eyes was something she could not hide. She could not deny that she knew that name. In fact, everyone in the county waiting on their court dates knew his name. He was only the very State's Attorney who headed all of the Assistant State's Attorneys in the county. His name was on everything in the state against violence and upholding the law. His name was in every newspaper and on every news station whenever there was a crime, so denying she knew who he was would be senseless.

"Your daddy's name is what? That is truly a fact you neglected to tell me while you were pillow talking everything else to me," Pandora retorted pacing the concrete cell floor in deep thought.

"I didn't tell you because I didn't want you to judge me."

"Judge you?" Pandora felt her voice grow louder and calmed herself so as to not cause a scene. "How could you think I would judge you? You didn't even give me a chance, sugar."

"When people find out who my dad is they immediately write me off like I'm some spoiled little rich kid and that couldn't be further from the truth. Not to mention they try to use me."

"Yeah, just you talking about your dad you talk differently."

"See. Ugh, I am who I am and I can't change that, Pandora. But if you want to get out of here he's the only one who can help us."

"Ox, you might be able to skate on outta here with a slap on the wrist but I'm in here for murder. That shit ain't going away easily."

"No, but he can at least get your bail dropped until your court date."

"Huh? You think a man like that is going to

be willing to help somebody like me just because I'm fucking his precious baby girl."

Oxy laughed briefly. "You have no idea what kind of man my dad is. He's not as innocent as the media makes him out to be. People think he's some kind of God but in actuality he's just like you or me. He's just smart enough not to get caught with it. That's all."

"Hmm. So...you told him about me?"

"Yep, he says we should be outta here by tomorrow."

"Damn that quick, huh? Shit I can't wait!" Pandora exclaimed cheesing from ear to ear. "Wait, what did you say to him? I thought you weren't ready to be back with him?"

"I told him I'd straighten up my ways if he got my case dropped and help you post bail. I've never told him that I wanted to change my life before so it just melted his heart," Oxy laughed sarcastically.

"Is that what you want to do, change your life?"

"Well I was thinking since we're getting married, we could settle down and create a family. I could get a job working under the table on cars or something and you can stay at home with the kids. You know, once you beat your case and all."

"Kids?" Pandora sneered. "Who said anything about kids?"

"You don't want kids? That's what married people do once they settle down right?"

"Okay, um, first thing's first. We need to get out and once we're out I need to go get my money."

"How much money are you worried about, Pandora? Cause I got money. I come from money," Oxy declared popping her collar.

"Close to fifty grand."

"Fifty grand, that's it? Girl my trust fund is worth more than that boo-boo," Oxy chuckled before looking up into the scorned eyes of her fiancé.

"It don't matter how much money it is. I earned it with blood, sweat and tears and the shit is fucking mine and I want it back. Okay?"

"Yeah, yeah. No problem baby. I didn't mean to upset you. I'm just saying I can give you fifty grand if you want it," Oxy digressed sliding her foot out of her mouth. "I meant it when I told you I could give you anything."

Pandora read in Oxy's eyes that she meant what she said. For a moment she felt bad about playing her. She had a good head game but she had to admit it was nowhere near comparable to Lexi's. There was something about the flutter of her tongue against her pearl that made her weak at the knees. It was the sweet caress of her smooth skin that made her body liquefy like putty on a warm summer day. As a tingly feeling overcame her she tore her gaze away from Oxy so as not to alert her that she was thinking of someone else. She licked her lips before gaining her composure to face her again.

"I know you meant it, Ox. But I ain't letting that shit go, not for a second. Those bitches played hardball when they took my money. I ain't just skipping town and forgetting about that shit," Pandora argued.

"Skip town? What you mean?"

"I don't think I'm gonna beat this case, Ox. If you are down for me then you gotta be down for whatever I'm doing."

"But I told my dad that—"

"But I love you baby," Pandora lied. "Don't you love me?"

"I know you don't love me Pandora. I may

be gullible when it comes to sweet, pretty pussy like yours but I'm not stupid."

Pandora walked over standing in front of Oxy allowing her stomach to brush up against her lips. She raised her prison blue shirt revealing a smooth surface belly that made Oxy salivate. The water filled up in her mouth faster than she could swallow it as she yearned for the need to devour her right then and there. Pandora grabbed and rubbed her hand around to the back of her head then smashed her face into her belly permitting Oxy to get a brief whiff of her bodily essence. Oxy stuck her tongue out tasting her salty flesh wanting to rip her clothes off and spread her open so badly.

Thump! Thump! Thump!

"Hey! What are you two doing in there?" A female officer said tapping their cell window with her black baton.

"Nothing, she was crying and I was just giving her a hug," Pandora was good at lying. It was so second nature to her that it just rolled off her tongue effortlessly.

"Yeah well separate before somebody thinks it's more than that," the officer yelled through the door before double checking then walking off.

Pandora backed off Oxy leaning against the

wall to satisfy those who spied on them for a living. She was beyond tired of the whole surveillance life and could not wait for the moment she was able to walk out of there a free woman. It was hard for her to fathom a life inside of those prison walls and thought it stupid for someone like Oxy to have chosen to be a career criminal. She had the good life, not like the upbringing Pandora and her sisters had. Oxy had it good and she was dumping it all in the trash for a chance to look cool to the people she used to run with. She envied her and considered her a disgrace all at the same time.

"I swear we can't leave here soon enough. I hate this place with a passion," Pandora sighed shaking her head.

"It's not so bad once you learn the rules."

"You shouldn't even be learning the rules. You are rich and your daddy is powerful. You're just crazy."

"Like I said, my dad is not all that people make him out to be alright. We don't even get along much. We're always butting heads but he just pacifies me so I'll be his prize child," Oxy spoke as she lowered her head.

"Shit, I wish someone would baby me so I would do right or go to college and buy me whatever I want. A trust fund, if I was a trust fund, baby trust that I wouldn't be caught dead in a place like this," Pandora recited snootily.

"Yeah well if you want my life so badly then take it."

"If only it was that damn simple," Pandora rolled her eyes. "Anyway when is he coming to get us?"

"He's not."

"What? Please don't tell me you fucking lied to me Oxy, I swear I will kill you dead right here."

"Is that a threat from the murderess, Pandora?" Oxy stood getting back on her thug stance. I don't take too kindly to idle threats."

"It ain't idle. But it wasn't a threat either. I'm just saying."

"Hmm. He's going to send a car for us in the morning. Said we should be released around dawn,"

"Cool. Well we'd better pack up our shit so we'll be ready. I can't wait."

"Uh, Pandora, there's just one more thing," Oxy turned grabbing her hand to slow her excitement. "We have to live with him until your case is closed."

"What? Why?"

"Because he wants to keep an eye on us and make sure we don't get into any more trouble. He's putting his rep on the line for us so he's not gonna tarnish that just cause I called in for him to rescue me."

It was something Pandora had not anticipated but she knew that at least she would be somewhere nobody would know. She was a grown woman and nobody was going to hold her prisoner again whether it be in a house or in a cell, she was determined not to be shackled. Swallowing the grief she felt about the whole situation and muscling up the strength to proceed, she shrugged her shoulders.

"No biggie, right? I mean what's the worse than can happen there? So we go out and do our business and come back in like we were looking for jobs or something." Pandora smiled.

"Yeah, I guess," Oxy shrugged squeezing her hand. "Do you really need that money from your sisters? Is it really that important to you?"

It was a question that she had replayed over and over in her head, wondering why Oxy could not understand her logic. The money was hers. She had worked so hard to get it and when she had it she felt like a queen, not needing or wanting anybody to do shit for her. She was able to stand on her own two feet like a boss when she had her money, never wanting to go back to broke. Being broke, people treated you like you were diseased and they looked at you with disrespect.

But what she truly wanted more than anything was revenge on the bitches that had put her in that predicament in the first place. She regretted not getting rid of them when she had the chance but the thought of killing Lexi at the time was more than she could bear. More than once she kicked herself in the ass for not planting a bullet in between Diamond's eyes but that was one mistake she knew she would not make again.

"Did I tell you I called Diamond the other day? I told that bitch I was coming for my money, so she knows she better have it ready," Pandora replied not getting totally off subject.

"You called her collect?"

"No. I sweet talked that cutie officer Jeff to use his cell. He was real sweet about it."

"I'm sure you did. Did you fuck him Pandora?" The anger in Oxy's eyes displayed a level of hell Pandora was unfamiliar with.

"Why do you always gotta jump to conclusions about shit, Ox? Damn!"

"Cause I know deep in your heart you are not all the way mines. I told you I'm not stupid, girl."

"Well you might not be stupid but you keep this shit up and you are most definitely gonna run me away. I can't deal with that kind of shit, straight up."

Oxy calmed down realizing she was right. Pandora was the only girl who did not think she was grotesque and who opened up to her when she needed it. Oxy liked to be needed and with her frail stature and lesbian ways, many sexy women in public did not want to give her the time of day but in jail she could find a carpet licking chick with no problem and no hesitation. It was part of the reason why she liked to stay in jail where her peers would not penalize her desires. Pandora was the most beautiful one she snagged though, and she was going to move hell and high water just to keep her as long as she abided by her rules.

"I'm sorry baby. I'm sorry," Oxy said moving close to her nibbling on her ear just how she liked, "You forgive me?"

Oxy moved her hand down inside of Pandora's elastic waist skirt, fiddling her pearl like she was strumming a guitar. Pandora tilted her head back exhaling intensely needing to release

some stress from their conversation. She
concentrated hard, focusing on the rapid
movements on her clit hoping she could cum
before anybody noticed what they were doing.

"Do it faster baby?" she exhaled grabbing
hold of her tits for increased pleasure.

"You like that shit baby?" Oxy breathed into
her ear feeling tiny drips drop down her legs.

"Faster bitch," Pandora answered pissed
that she was not following her directions.

"Naw you'll get more when we leave
tomorrow. I just thought I'd give you a small
taste."

Pandora respired in disgust ready to slap
the smile off of Oxy's face. She took her orgasms
very seriously and was sick of her half assed
attempts to please her anyway. The sneaking was
getting played and her head game seemed to be
falling off leaving Pandora horny and frustrated. If
looks could kill, she would have slaughtered her
right on that prison bunk bed. Her thoughts ran
rampant but she calmed down long enough to
focus on the big picture. It was only a matter of
hours before they would be released and all
Pandora could think about was getting what she
deserved. Nothing or no one else mattered.

Chapter 7: "Cause whether you open it or not it's still going to read the same information baby." — Nikki

Kojack sat on the let out couch in his office thinking about the events of the past few weeks. It was early. The sun had not crept across the sky yet but the fog alerted him that the hour of sunrise was upon him. He knew he was bogus for ignoring the millions of calls over the past few days from Lexi but he did not know another way to tear his self from her grasp. She was jailbait and that could only lead to one place, which was the one place he was trying to avoid besides his unexpected trip to the hospital. But even if he could get past that fact, he did not know if he could trust that Lexi was telling the truth about not sleeping with Diamond. Diamond's words were programmed in his head like a DVR player and it was hard for him to let them go.

He pulled out the short rectangular folded up piece of paper that the doctor had given him and stared down at it like it was diseased. It was the one thing that held his fate and he could not bring his self to read the results. Every day since he left the hospital he had been dreading reading the words on the small sliver of paper but he knew eventually he needed to do so. It should not have been that hard for him since he goes to the doctor regularly for checkups and tests but it truly hit home for him when he knew that it could very well be a great possibility. The very possibility of him having a disease inside of him that he would not be able to take a few pills for and flush out of his system scared him shitless. It was incurable, it was deadly, and it was fatale.

His long arm reached over for another bottle of Corona from the box of long necks that he had purchased. He cracked it open with the opener on his keys and tossed the cap on the floor to join the other dozens that were already there with their bottle counterparts. The office was a mess and he smelled a fright having not washed his body even though his office adorned a full marble cabinet bathroom that he built his self. It had a huge closet full of clothes that he had placed in there for days much like the ones he had been spending there along with a full washer and dryer but Kojack had not felt like doing anything since he had the news of his HIV test results in his hand.

"Boss...oh I'm sorry," Nikki, his assistant said as she barged in on him in his plaid boxers and white tank top.

"Naw, Naw it's cool. Come on in. What do you need Nikki?" he mumbled his words slurred.

"Um, I just wanted to give you these invoices. They needed to be signed before I could mail them off," Nikki said looking around the office bewildered as to why it looked like a trash can exploded inside of it. "Do you wanna talk or something?"

"Talk about what, the fact that my life is slowly going to shit or the fact that the weight of the world is on my shoulders?"

Nikki sat her thick dark skinned waist down on the bed next to him. Her four inch boots remained on the floor so she did not get any dirt in the bed out of respect for him. Her jeans were extra tight and her blouse remained unbuttoned one button below normal everyday just for a man who never paid attention to her. She flicked her shoulder length hair and batted her dark brown eyes at him hoping he was sobbing because of a break up. She was an expert at making men feel better.

"Why don't you start at the beginning, baby? I'm here for you," she cooed while rubbing his leg gently.

"What's the point? It won't change what's written on this piece of paper."

"Let me see the paper."

"No. I need to be a man and do this on my own. Could you just leave and shut the door and tell no one else to come in here. I'm not working today," Kojack said leaning back on the back of the sofa.

"I really don't think you should be alone right now sweetie. I mean, look at you. Have you even bathed?" Nikki said running her fingers across the top of his braided hair.

"Naw, gotta do this first."

"Well whenever you're ready just open it. Cause whether you open it or not it's still going to read the same information baby," Nikki replied standing to give him a good view of her backside, "Call me if you need me sweetie. You know I'm here for you."

"Speaking of being here, why are you here so damn early? Site workers don't get here 'til 7 a.m."

"I always get a head start on my days."

"So you start early and leave late all in the interest of the company?" Kojack questioned.

"It's something like that," Nikki winked as she walked out of the door shutting it gently behind her.

Kojack nodded her off knowing exactly what she wanted. He could not even fathom thinking about something like that with the information he needed revealed to him on a single sheet of paper. He his self could not understand what was taking him so long to unravel this sheet and read the results. The thought of his life being decided by this test was not something he was prepared to deal with. As he sat back staring off into nothing he began to realize the root of his problems began with Diamond. As many times as he avoided females like her, he kicked his self repeatedly for finally giving in.

"Shit! I can't change shit now, man. But I didn't fuck her though. I know I didn't fuck her," He recited over and over to his self, "Did I fuck her?"

He was confused. He could not figure out if he had slept with Diamond thinking she was Pandora or vice versa. They played so many games back then and they looked so very much alike that hell, they could have been the same person if it were not for their different personalities. It was a trait that he learned too late in the game. He placed his head in both of his hands rubbing his eyes roughly attempting to relieve stress from them as the paper slid out of his hand and onto the bed. It fell slightly open and when he looked up to find it he saw wording peeping out from inside. Curiosity sunk in and his fingers grew a mind of their own as he reached for it flapping it open with one hand finally laying his eyes on the contents within.

****

Blagh! Blagh!

Lexi wiped her mouth and flushed the toilet cleaning the remaining upchucks off of the floor with tissue. She ran the cold water in the sink, cuffing her hand under the flow to splash a bit of it in her mouth. After the initial feeling subsided she grabbed her toothbrush and began scrubbing away the awful taste that still lingered orally.

"Hey Lex, you okay in there? It's too early in the morning to be crying over Kojack now. Come on out of there," Diamond yelled from the other side of the bathroom door.

She tried the knob but Lexi had made sure to lock it behind her. Lexi had never felt this way before and the only thing that rolled through her mind was Diamond's words, she had AIDS. Her heart beat faster and harder than a bass drum at a parade as she tried not to hyperventilate. All of her promiscuity was fun and fulfilling but she slowly began to comprehend that it all came with a cost, even though it was a day late and a dollar short.

"I'm good, Diamond. Just go away, okay," Lexi shooed the door as if it were she.

"No I'm not going anywhere until you open this damn door, because I know you ain't good," Diamond banged harder on the white wooden door.

"Ugh just go the fuck away!"

"NO!"

"Dammit Diamond," Lexi roared as she turned the lock and whisked open the door. "Motherfuckas need privacy sometimes, damn."

"Whatever. What's going on in here?" Diamond asked raising her bony arm to stroke her sister's hair but found it batted away.

"Don't touch me. I don't want to be touched right now," Lexi growled mean mugging her own face in the oversized square bathroom mirror.

"Hey don't get snappy at me just cause you mad your man ain't been home. I don't know what to tell you. Shit fuck him, girl. We need to be focused on squaring up with that bitch ass sister of yours."

"She's your sister too Diamond."

"Yeah, but only by blood, fuck that ho. The sooner you start thinking like that the better off you'll be."

Lexi could feel the chunks rise to the top of her throat once more. She breathed heavily trying to force herself to hold it back and be okay but it seemed like it was coming no matter how much she fought. She spooned her hands underneath the running water again and puts water in her mouth hoping for relief. It was there. The water forced the vomit back down her throat and into her stomach as slight cramps began to form at the top of her abdomen. She soon realized as the pain increased that swallowing the vomit was a big mistake.

"Well I got business to take care of. You can stay here and wallow in your own shit but I ain't gonna stick around to watch," Diamond said as she walked off, "I'll be back tonight."

"Diamond..." Lexi whispered as she listened to her footsteps become more and more distant, "Diamond!"

The pain in her stomach was now becoming more than she could bear. It was unbelievable that mere vomit was the cause of the growing agony in her body. Lexi began to think of what she could have done to deserve such punishment from God.

Her next thoughts were to ask Him to take her home now because she was not a person who could suffer through pain especially if she was going to die. Again, Diamond's words rang true in her head. She did not know much about AIDS, just that you could get it through sex and it was obviously incurable, but she knew that if pain was what she had to go through she would just as well kill herself before enduring it.

"Diamond!" Lexi yelled again now balled up on the floor helplessly.

"What the fuck are you..." Diamond kneeled down to her stroking her hair gently, "Oh my God, Lex. Lex, baby what's wrong? Are you okay? Lex, Oh my God! Come on baby you have to get up so we can get you to a hospital."

"No...no hospitals, just take me to a clinic. I'll be good."

"Bitch ain't nobody about to sit in a shabby ass clinic waiting on a low budget ass doctor to tell you to take some Tylenol and call it a day. You need a real doctor and we're going to the fucking hospital. Now get up!" Diamond demanded wrapping her arm around Lexi's torso and helping her to her feet.

"Aight, forget it. I think I'll be fine. I just need to drink some water or something. Shit, maybe it's my period coming on."

"No period does you like that, Lex. I ain't stupid. I told you to take your ass to the fucking doctor and get checked out."

"Man, ain't no fucking doctor gonna tell me I got AIDS and shit. The fucking plague and shit! Ain't no doctor gonna tell me I'm gonna die, yo!" Lexi cried nearly becoming weak in the knees, "I'm sorry Diamond. But I don't wanna die."

Boulders of tears rolled from Lexi's big brown eyes and onto her golden brown cheeks as she shoved her short hair back behind her ears. It was almost as if Lexi knew her life was already over. Her illness coupled with depression from Kojack's separation from her began to be more than she could stand. She could hardly breathe feeling like her heart was about to stop and her blood would cease to flow. There was something wrong but she could not pinpoint exactly what.

Diamond sighed as she rushed to help Lexi with her coat and then out of the door into the car. "Don't worry about it Lex. I know it can be a scary thing. But like you said boo, life must go on."

"I don't know if I'm as strong as you D."

"You are you just don't know it yet. Listen, you are going to be fine and you're going to be a great aunt and be able to teach my kid...everything I couldn't," Diamond brushed a finger gently against Lexi's face. "Okay? So quit freakin' out and let's get you to this hospital to find out what's wrong."

Lexi nodded. It was all she could do as she worked to calm herself and think happy thoughts. The pain seemed to grow by the minute sending striking sharp pains through her stomach and around to her back forcing her to squirm in her seat. It felt as if a sharp knife was plunging inside of her, penetrating her organs over and over again trying for death. As Diamond drove down the street like she was racing for cash, she could not help but cringe every time Lexi grimaced with pain.

"Please hurry, D. I can't take it! I can't take it anymore!"

Chapter 8: "Never. I got you, baby." — Pandora

"It's fucking freezing out here. They could have at least given us a coat or something in this bitch," Pandora noted through her chattering teeth.

"Fuck all that. I'm just happy to breathe fresh smog filled air rather than a piss infested cell," Oxy rebutted.

"Either way it goes you motherfuckas will be back. Mark my words," The female correctional officer said snickering and sliding her hands into her oversized cop issued winter coat.

The women turned facing the blank open road rolling their eyes in disgust. They prayed the officer would just go back inside of the gate and leave them be. Oxy's dad had come through on his end of the bargain and they were indeed as free as a bird but were patiently waiting for a car to pick them up. The ladies both had on regular jeans and t-shirts accept Oxy adorned K-Swiss gym shoes and Pandora wore Christian Louboutin, the very shoes she went in the jail with.

"Where the fuck is this car? I can't stand out here like this anymore," Pandora whined, folding her arms to keep herself warm.

"Quit your crying. My dad said he was sending a car then he'll send…"

A shiny black Lincoln Town car that had eased up parking in front of them interrupted Oxy's words. She knew it was for them because her dad always sent black cars with dark tinted windows whenever it had anything to do with her. It was almost as if he was ashamed of her. Pandora tiptoed happily towards the car anxious to rip the door open and jump inside to warmth.

Ivan Smear jumped out of the car too anxious to see them. He stood six feet tall hovering over the ladies like the Sears Tower. His smile resembled a devilish clown as it shined bright from ear to ear. He was lanky but held his physique intact as Pandora watched his muscles bulge through his tailor made, button down, striped collar shirt. Forget State's Attorney, in her mind he looked like a bodybuilding champion. His green eyes and creamy white skin gave way to the typical Caucasian male but his dark, jet black hair and sultry stance made him look like he was fresh out of a GQ Magazine.

"Ah, if it isn't my dear, sweet, daughter Oxy, hello baby," Ivan smiled as he walked up to them with open arms, shooing Pandora in the car quickly, "Well aren't you going to give your dear old dad a hug?"

"Hey Ivan," Oxy mumbled as he pulled her in close for a welcoming hug.

"Well let's get the hell outta here huh," Ivan chuckled escorting her into the front seat of the car.

"I didn't think you were going to personally pick us up yourself," Oxy said staring over at Pandora yet addressing her dad.

"I wouldn't have it any other way. I couldn't have my only baby girl out here scrimmaging for a ride up North now could I?" Ivan responded watching Pandora with a close eye through the rear view mirror.

Pandora looked over at Oxy wondering what was wrong with her. Her whole demeanor changed once Ivan stepped out of the car to greet her. There was tension in the air but truthfully she could care less about the issues her and her dad faced with each other. Being able to view the orange and blue morning sky as a free woman was all she concerned herself with at that point.

"So Pandora, murder huh, that's quite the doozy don't you think?" Ivan's words rolled off his tongue sarcastically. "Don't worry. I'm sure we can get you off with a self-defense plea."

"Yeah, he was trying to rape me and my sisters. I had no choice."

"Why didn't you go to the police?"

"Because, it's hard to call the police when you've got a big, shiny black ass gun being toted in your face," Pandora responded sarcastically.

"Ah, I see you're a potty mouth little girl huh?" Ivan smirked eyeing her through the rearview mirror, "I know just how to handle potty mouths."

"Dad, let's just drop it okay?" Oxy said shaking her head and refocusing her eyes on the outdoor scenery.

"Oh Oxy, you know your old man doesn't like a potty mouth."

"Yes but we are grown women so none of that applies to us."

Pandora sat studying both of their demeanors from the back seat as the car drove on in complete and utter silence. There was something strange about them but she could not put her finger on it. She wanted to engage in conversation and address his remark with a quick sly yet educated comment, but something in her gut just told her to let it go. Instead she chose to stare blankly out the window at the beautiful, bright orange sunrise. Thirty minutes later they pulled up into the driveway of Ivan and Oxy's luxury 2 story

home. They all exited the car with Oxy walking
further ahead, quickly making her way up to the
wooden door with a stained glass center. The
house was not huge at all it seemed from the
outside, in the small Bolingbrook suburb, but once
they entered, Pandora felt like she was in a
miniature paradise.

"We'll be in my room if you need us," Oxy
said quickly snatching Pandora's hand attempting
to head up the long staircase.

"I'll be in my office. I need to talk to your
friend there about her case if I'm going to get her
off," Ivan said shutting the door and walking past
the ladies disappearing into the darkness behind
the stairs.

"Wait," Pandora gasped as she snatched her
hand back. "Let me look around a bit damn."

"Ugh. It's just a regular old crummy house.
Well when you're done, I'll be upstairs," Oxy
turned in disgust at her gawking.

Pandora could not even focus on her rude
departure having been so engulfed in the beauty of
the house. The curtains on the windows looked like
they were Victorian inspired, as did the plush sofas
to her left and mahogany wood dining set to her
right. The walls were all filled with various
paintings and family portraits as if they were once

a beautiful loving family, as if the now cold and dark house once had life inside. Right at the foot of the stairs was a huge picture of a beautiful dark haired woman. Her eyes were mystical reminding her of that of her own mother's. Breaking her gaze before she turned emotional, she stared down the dark hall Ivan dissolved down wondering what was beyond the blackness. She could only imagine what the kitchen looked like, her most favorite part of any house.

Done with the shock and awe tour, her feet made their way up the long stairwell and down the picture framed filled hallway to a well lit room at the end, Oxy's room. She pushed the door open to find a huge lovely room full of anything and everything that had to do with the color pink. From the carpet to the paint, the entire room blinded her by the presence of the hue. It was amazingly clean and her king size bed adorned a shimmering pink spread across it. There were huge bay windows that Oxy left open allowing the sunlight to dance into the room. The doors to her walk in closet were agape revealing an astonishing array of clothing that she could not wait to sink her claws into.

"Bitch, you live in a fucking mansion and get anything you want, a trust fund? I wish I had some shit like that," Pandora blurted as she turned to the fifty-inch screen TV mounted on the wall attractively, "Maybe I wouldn't be in the shit I'm in now…"

"Well if you want it, you can have it," Oxy replied slipping her jeans off then hopping on the bed in only her tattered white t-shirt and dingy panties.

"Ewe."

"What?" Oxy sucked her teeth, "Awe girl please, like you've never chilled with your sisters in your shirts and panties before."

"Yeah but…never mind. So anyway I would take it off your hands but there's only one problem, I'm not related to you!" Pandora laughed with her.

"Man, fuck this shit. The only reason why I care about this shit is so I can take care of you once we're married, that's it. If I never met you ain't no telling where I'd be."

"Yeah" Pandora hesitated. "The wedding is gonna happen just as soon as I get some shit in order.

"Humph."

"What? What the hell does that mean?"

"Nothing Pandora."

"No, you obviously have something to say. So spit it out."

"I'm just wondering why settling scores is the only thing on your mind when I was the one to get you out of jail and I am the one you are supposed to be marrying. You ain't even appreciative of that shit," Oxy growled. "I thought you would at least try to focus on the wedding."

"God, why does it always have to be about that with you? I said we would get to it so we'll get to it. Can we just breathe and smell fresh air before we do anything?"

"Air, bitch you were the one who brought up the whole marriage shit in the first place…unless you were just using me to get what you wanted," Oxy exclaimed.

Even though she knew the answer she just wanted to see if Pandora had the balls to say it. If she did not then it meant that she had a tiny bit of love and enough respect for her not to break her heart or hurt her feelings. But if she came out putting her intentions on full blast then she knew Pandora was only out for self and could care less about her. Lies she could deal with since she was a master of them and had gone through life living them. She tucked her hands under her legs to keep the sweat from dripping from them as she leaned in with interest awaiting the answer she would speak.

"Ugh!" Pandora sighed in hatred as she rolled her eyes and plopped down on the bed, "No, I'm not using you Oxy. I just need to focus on tying up loose ends. Is that cool with you?"

"Yeah, I guess it's cool," Oxy breathed relieved from the lie Pandora told.

"You guess?"

"Yeah, I guess. I'm just saying; try not to lose sight of the main objective for getting out of jail. You know what I'm saying?"

"Never, I got you babe," Pandora played her card, moving in to seductively stroke her chin with her fingernail just the way Oxy liked it.

"Naw you ain't got me yet, but you will," Oxy said laying Pandora down on the bed pressing her lips to hers.

"Mmm, wait. This is great and all and trusts I want my pussy licked badly especially after all that damn sneaking and shit. But baby you need to get your stanky ass in the fucking shower," Pandora giggled as she slowly slid out from under her.

"What? You ain't never minded my smell

before. Now cause we here you wanna act brand new."

"Shit, I've always had a problem with it. Why do you think I always ask you to brush your teeth before you eat my pussy? Being locked up is one thing but we're free now bitch, so go clean yourself."

Oxy dismounted her and headed into the bathroom connected to her room. She headed straight for the small corner shower turning the water on not even giving it a chance to warm up before stepping inside. As she lathered up she began to daydream about the married life with Pandora having two kids and a dog in a nice quiet suburban life. She would be the perfect mom to her kids that her mom never was to her and ensure that no harm ever came to them. She thought about giving her wife and kids any and everything they wanted and could not wait to be able to do so to see the smiles on their faces. Once she was done she quickly grabbed a huge, blue beach towel from the nearby rack then dried the tiny water droplets stuck to her skin.

"Ha! I'm so fresh and so clean," Oxy said flinging open the door and jumping out as naked as the day she was born.

To her disappointment, she found a fast

asleep Pandora curled up in a ball on the bed with the covers pulled almost to her head. She walked over to see if she was really sleeping and found that she was not only sleeping but also snoring as well. With her head hung low she pimped around to the other side of the bed and slid underneath the covers with her. Oxy wrapped her bony arms around Pandora's waist spooning her closely, placing tiny pecks on the back of her neck. She leaned in laying her head close to hers then closed her eyes grinning and happy to have such a beautiful body lying in front of her.

Chapter 9: "So because he didn't respect you, you killed him?" — *Ivan*

"Awe shit!" Kojack bellowed as he read the results on the paper.

His heart knocked louder than the storm brewing outside of his office window. Never in his life had he been so nervous or scared of something even with knowing how unavoidable it was. He rose from the sofa bed ready to tear the paint off the walls and scream to the top of his lungs. A knock at the door startled him from his gaze at the paper. It was the type of knock that had quickly turned into a police type of banging as his heart jumped up out of his shirt the closer he moved towards the door.

"WHAT?" he yelled as he yanks the door open.

"Um, I'm sorry Kojack but there is someone on the phone for you who say it's a matter of life and death," Nikki said handing him the company's cordless phone that she carried around the site often.

"Didn't I tell you I didn't want any calls?"

"I understand sweetie but they said it was

life or death and I didn't know if it was someone from your family or not. I didn't want to take any risks if it was something very serious," Nikki rebutted insisting he take the phone from her hand with a shoving gesture.

Kojack reluctantly snatched the phone from her hands and turned to take the call. He put the receiver to his earlobe without uttering a peep hoping to listen to the background noise to figure out who it was on the other end. He slowed his breathing so the person would not know that he was on the phone listening in. For the most part, there was very little noise in the background that he could identify with and pinpoint a person or location. He twiddled his nose a bit as he stared back at Nikki who was standing there either patiently waiting for the phone or being nosey. Either way it ticked him off.

"Yo who is this?" Kojack spoke authoritatively.

"Nigga this is Diamond. Who the fuck else you thought it was? You don't know my fucking number by now?"

"Oh, guess I wasn't expecting a call from you so I wasn't paying attention. So what you want?"

"Damn it's like that now? Check it, ya girl is

in the hospital. I'm here with her now but I got some things I need to take care of."

"Well what's wrong with her?"

"They don't know yet Kojack. They are waiting for the test results to come back. The doctor said it should be within the hour."

"Well if she's still alive then she's alright then right?" Kojack asked.

"Look, I know you and her broke up and shit but she needs you. The least you could do is act like you once gave a damn," Diamond growled.

Kojack sighed knowing he may have been acting unreasonable, "Where she at man?"

"I drove her to the city to Christ Hospital. They're the best at trauma situations and I didn't want to leave my sister's life in the hands of some second rate Resident."

"Aight man, I'll be there in minute."

"Well your company is right up the street so it should barely take you that. She really does need you."

"Ay, don't rush me. You talking about she needs me, but what about you? Huh? Why are you leaving?"

"I just got some business I need to handle. That's all."

"Diamond, what business could be more important than your family?"

Diamond stewed for a minute on the thought. It never ran through her mind that her leaving could quite possibly be wrong on her part but she felt if she did not tear herself apart from the hospital early she would never be able to.

"Nigga, can you just bring your ass up to this damn hospital and be with your damn girl. I don't even know what you all broke up for. You know you in love with the damn girl, shit," Diamond spat evading the question.

"Jeez. Aight, I'll be there in a few."

With those words Kojack hung up the phone. He was not the least bit interested in continuing on in conversation with her since she was the initiating cause of all of his heartache and grief. He was perfectly fine with his life until she came in disrupting it with her incurable disease. His world was stomped on, confused, and turned upside down because of it and the very thought of having to see her face again fucked his head up. Nonetheless, he walked to the bathroom turning the shower on then headed back to the office to escort Nikki out so he could get dressed in private.

"Here, take this phone girl. If I say I don't want no calls I mean no calls. You got it? If it ain't my momma, fuck the world. You understand?" Kojack spoke firmly.

"Yes. Yes I understand."

"Thanks. Now if you'll excuse me, I need to get dressed," Kojack raised his hand to give her the gesture to leave.

"Asshole," Nikki mumbled.

"What did you just say?"

"Huh? What?"

"Don't play coy with me. I heard you say something. Be a woman and spit it out."

Nikki sighed annoyingly, "If you must know, I called you an asshole…sir."

"Why? Why am I the asshole?"

"Because Kojack, I have been working for you for three years now and I don't get any attention at all. I daydream every day about us being together. I handle all your business when you're not here, holding it down for you. I'm your shoulder to cry on, your cook when you need it, your nurse, and I'm every woman for you. But you don't know a good woman when you see her.

You'd rather run up behind whores all day."

"Nikki, why must we go through this again? I wish I had never fucked you that night two years ago. We were drunk and you're reading into it, making it something it's not. It was just drunk sex. That's it."

"See that's exactly what I mean. Yeah it was drunken sex but you're not even thinking about what could've grown from that or how long I was in your corner before then. You just use females for your own personal gain. You don't give a fuck about nobody but yourself," Nikki's facial expression went from distraught to pissed in under a minute.

"I do care...ugh. Nikki, I never said I didn't care about you. I'm just in a really weird time in my life right now and it's fucking with me."

"Yeah, well so am I, Kojack. But I refuse to let it fuck with me any longer. I love you. Can you say that you love me too?" Nikki asked walking up to him preparing for a kiss if he decided to deliver one.

"Love, are you sure?" Kojack already knew the answer gazing down into her eyes. "I...I..."

"That's what I thought," Nikki mumbled, as she turned headed for the door. "Consider this my thirty day notice."

"Shit!" Kojack blurted as she slammed his office door.

He did not have time for that shit from her. She had threatened to leave a couple of times before when he refused to commit to her but she never did. This time seemed no different. He headed for the closet to pick out a simple white tee and a pair of Sean Jean jeans to wear for the day with some wheat colored Timberlands and dashed into the shower. The only thing he could wrap his head around after that was if there was something really wrong with Lexi or was she playing yet another one of her games. He felt if it was a game, it would be one that he wasn't in the mood for and she would dearly pay for her actions this time. Kojack walked around cleaning the room before he headed out the door.

*****

Pandora awoke with the warm sunrays beating across her face. She sat up noticing she was entangled in Oxy's embrace. She wiggled her waist out of it slyly, careful not to wake her up noticing the time on the Hello Kitty clock mounted on the

wall next to the oversized, big screen TV. It read
8:32 am, which puzzled her because it did not feel
like she was asleep that long. After stretching as
long as she could and gazing out the window at
the wildly huge backyard beyond the balcony, she
turned to find Oxy staring back at her eerily.

Pandora breathed rolling her eyes, "So what
can I wear and where's the bathroom?"

"Pick whatever you want that's in the closet,
I don't care. Bathroom's through there," Oxy
replied casually thumbing through her hair.

"You have your own fucking bathroom? Oh
your ass is spoiled and ungrateful for real,"
Pandora turned her head in the direction she was
pointing, feeling the sense of shock overcome her
again.

"Whatever," Oxy retorted grabbing her IPod
from the pink end table and plugging her ears,
"Hey after you get out of there we need to talk
about what we're gonna do for the wedding."

"What? Oh yeah right. Sure," Pandora
crossed her eyes as she burrowed through her
wardrobe for a black baby doll tunic and a pair of
skinny jeans that were surprisingly her size,
despite Oxy's frail frame.

Oxy was so busy rocking out to the loud

heavy metal music penetrating her ears that she had not even heard a word from Pandora. She shook her head at the troubled girl and headed into the bathroom, which was not as luxurious as her room was. It held a small shower, toilet and sink with a well-lit vanity mirror above it. She rested the clothes on the top of the sink then opened the glass door to the shower turning the hot water knob and removing her clothes in the process. Stepping lightly into the rising steamed shower she began to think about her sisters. They were disloyal ass bitches that broke the code. They broke the covenant; the bond they had established between themselves and now it was time for them to pay the piper.

As she lathered up, she realized that they were her only witness to the crime she had committed. In her mind, without witnesses the police had nothing and the prosecution had no case. It was time to axe those bitches once and for all. Her adrenaline rushed through her veins as she turned the water off and reached for a hanging bath towel to dry off. After dressing, she toweled off her damp hair and headed back into Oxy's room only to find her fast asleep with the music still blaring through the headphones.

The time on the pink Hello Kitty clock read 9:15 am. Pandora thought the good State's

Attorney might have been tucked away in his warm bed trying to recoup the sleep he lost but figured she would venture downstairs just to see. If nothing else it would give her an excuse to see the rest of the house's splendor. On the first floor, she headed down the short hall and into the kitchen. It was then that she understood why the house did not look big from the outside. Most of the house was swallowed up by the living and dining room leaving a rather miniscule area for the kitchen. It was cute and compact with a nice floral pattern on the walls and stainless steel black appliances but it was indeed the smallest room in the house next to Oxy's personal bathroom.

"Ah, I see you didn't forget. I like that in a client. One who can remember to do what I ask of them," Ivan appeared out of the darkness behind her.

"Oh my God!" Pandora gasped clenching her chest. "Where the hell did you come from? You scared the shit out of me."

"My office is this way," he laughed walking past her through a doorway in the kitchen.

"You have a lovely hou— uh, home," Pandora stumbled over her words as she followed him into the back room.

She looked around at his office, snarling. It

had a file cabinet, a small wooden desk covered in papers and an HP laptop, and what appeared to be a combination safe peeking out from behind the desk. The medium sized room almost looked like that of a playroom for children or a pet. It was not ideal at all to her and it began to make her wonder what kind of lawyer he was that he was the best in the city but he lived almost like he was broke. Nonetheless, Pandora could not take her mind or eyes off of that safe. She was itching to know the contents inside.

"I know what you're thinking," he began as he took a sip from his glass half filled with a dark brown substance. "Would you like some?"

"Uh no thanks, isn't it a little early to be drinking, if you don't mind me saying so?"

"It's never too early for a drink, love," Ivan smirked eyeballing her, "Have a seat."

Pandora looked around the room noticing there were no windows or any other kind of ventilation in the room. It looked as if he had merged a simple hall closet and kitchen closet into one to make his office. The only light hung from the ceiling, but he made sure to keep bright light bulbs in it to illuminate the entire room with no problem. She was uncomfortable in there not because of him but because she thought she was going to hyperventilate from claustrophobia.

"You're thinking, why doesn't this man have a luxurious house and why doesn't he drive a big fancy car? Am I right?" Ivan continued.

"Uh no, no sir I was thinking that you have a lovely home," Pandora smiled.

"Liar, you know I can tell a liar right. Like the back of my hand."

It was clear to Pandora that he had a few too many of those bourbons like the one in his hand. He sat the glass down on the desk remembering to use a coaster, before plopping down in his oversized computer chair. He swiveled just a tad bit before resting his elbows on his desk gazing down at the assortment of papers.

"So tell me what you were really thinking," he smirked.

Pandora took a deep breath, "Ugh, I was thinking that if the State's Attorney should at least be living a little hotter than this. Instead of like a pauper."

"A pauper huh, hmm nice word, I see someone is as intelligent and as stupid as my daughter," Ivan laughed, "And for your information, I don't live like a pauper because obviously I have more than you. Anyway my wife and I agreed that we'd spend our money wisely, that way we could retire early and comfortably."

"Wait, excuse me? Are you trying to call me dumb?"

"Well, you live your life like a smart, dumb criminal. You have the beauty and the brains but you choose to do absolutely nothing with it."

"Oh, I do something with it, Mr. Smear."

"Ivan. Please call me Ivan."

"Well I'm not dumb, Ivan. There's a whole lot of shit I know how to do."

"Really? Interesting. Then tell me your story. Why are the police charging you with murder?" Ivan leaned in on his desk awaiting her answer.

As Pandora spilled out what actually happened that faithful night Sun lost his life, she could not help but get the feeling he had already heard or somehow knew the story already. She ended and the room filled with air. He stared at her awkwardly but oddly enough she was not uncomfortable.

"So because he didn't respect you, you killed him?" Ivan asked taking another sip of his drink.

"No he's dead because he rapes women and then throws money at them to shut them up," Pandora snapped.

"But was it your place to judge him? You took the law into your own hands without even giving him his day in court."

"He would've gotten off!"

"How do you know that?" Ivan yelled back banging his hands on the desk, shooting her a stern eye.

It was the first time that she realized the severity of what she had done. It had finally set in to her feeble little brain that she could actually go to jail and do time for her anger, for her actions on that night. Apart of her was scared while another part of her wanted to flee the country. But she had no money and the cops seized the little money she had left. Her thoughts ran crazily in her mind as she stood there staring at the drunken lawyer waste his life away at the bottom of another glass.

"Oh my God," she gasped, "What am I going to do?"

"I'll tell you what we're going to do. We're going to go in there and tell them it was self-defense. Then you're going to pretend that you are indeed the sweet, young lady that we are going to dress you up to be and gain sympathy from the judge."

"Do you think you can get me off, Ivan?" The sweet tone in her voice made Ivan double back to check and make sure she was the same person.

"I'm gonna damn well try young lady. As a matter of fact I believe I can keep this thing from going to trial."

"Oh my God! Are you serious? That would be so...I would forever be in your debt if you did," Pandora batted her eyes, "So, I'm just curious, what did happen to your wife?"

"Ah yes the so-called love of my life. Well, she got tired of me cheating, tired of the long trips away from home and tired of the lonely nights. So now I'm the one with the lonely drunken nights," he said realizing there was no more liquor in the bottle for him to pour into his glass, "All I have to pacify the fact that her mother abandoned us for a twenty five year old Latin bastard and is now fucking him on a beach somewhere, not even thinking about us, is this good old glass."

"Oh wow, I'm so sorry!" Pandora covered her mouth.

There were no other words Pandora could say after that. She felt for the man and knew that was the whole reason for his self-medicating. It was that that attracted her forcing her to rise from the chair and venture over to his desk. He leaned back in the chair interlocking his fingers and gawking at the young girl standing in front of him. His eyes showed signs of tears but his pride refused to permit them to appear.

"I'm so sorry."

"Eh. It is what it is. It's been over two and a half years now. You can't make the heart do what the heart doesn't want to do," he shuffled a few papers on his desk fighting back his pain.

"Have you thought about moving on with your life and finding someone new, someone that can make you happy?"

"Oh gee, Pandora. I don't know why I didn't think of that," Ivan smirked rolling his eyes.

"I'm just saying, maybe you need someone to take your mind off of her. It doesn't have to be someone you love just someone you love at that moment. You get what I'm saying?" she bent over slightly staring into his beady eyes.

"Yeah I get it. I need to go out and buy me a whore."

"You wouldn't have to buy one if you just fixed yourself up a bit. I mean look at you. What woman is going to want a sloppy drunk man? The only thing you have going for you is that you have money and your name. But that's not enough," Pandora retorted watching as he nearly passed out with his head hunched over to the side.

"I can't do it," Ivan slurred, "I'm not ready."

Pandora lowered her head then turned around prepared to leave. Her feet stepped on a few pieces of paper that had flown onto the floor from the pile. She bent to pick them up and could not help but to be nosey and read them. They were quickly snatched away, leaving her dizzy from the quickness. Brushing it off, Pandora looked over at his glowing brown skin as she headed towards the seat he fell in.

"Ivan. Ivan," she called but all she got in return were grunting noises.

She climbed on top of his lap slowly, one leg at a time then leaned in to kiss the man on his lips; they were soft and sweet tasting from the liquor. Her opening throbbed, as she had longed for a powerful piece to drive into her for weeks. He was not her ideal candidate to relieve her stress but her body needed it and from hearing Ivan's situation his body needed it to. Pandora saw it as doing a favor for a friend; after all, he was providing her with free grade a counsel and he genuinely wanted to help her. She nibbled at his neck then made her way back up to his lips while she attempted to unbutton his pants. The thought of Oxy's words never entered her mind.

"Hey...hey. What are you doing?" Ivan whispered oscillating his head from left to right trying to snap out of his drunken coma.

"Shh. Don't worry, momma's gonna take good care of you," Pandora assured between pecks on his neck.

"Mmm, no, I need you to stop," Ivan breathed.

"You like this baby?"

"Stop..."

"I can't wait to slide down your —"

"OFF!" Ivan stood up as she slid to the floor.

He seemed to be suffering palpitations heavily, trembling at every limb. Ivan ran his ringers across his hair panicking and hoping that Oxy could not hear what was going on in their house. His eyes scoured the room while Pandora peeled herself from the floor totally confused and adorning a shitty look on her face. She was obviously upset but a part of him did not care.

"I need you to go," Ivan cringed still searching the room with his eyes frenziedly. "I need you to go, now!"

"What the fuck did I do? I was only trying to help you?" Pandora pleaded.

"No you belong to...I am old belong to...ugh, please just leave."

"I just thought it would be nice if we could make each other feel good. You know help each other get over our problems," Pandora replied seductively as she removed her shirt, revealing a nice set of perky brown tits enveloped in a lace purple bra.

"No girl! Don't you understand? Here let me fucking help you!" Ivan pulled his desk drawer open and pulled out a .38 pointing it right at her. "I need you to leave now!"

"Ha, ha, you couldn't hurt me. You couldn't hurt a fly. You don't have it in you. It's gonna take a lot more than that to scare me, sugar. But don't get your panties in a bunch, I'll leave. But you will regret not hitting this ass later," Pandora blew a kiss at him then left the office heading back upstairs.

In the room, she laid on the floor, staring up at the ceiling as the heavy metal music finally died and the IPod cycled itself down. It may have been pretty forward for her to come at him that way but she did not care. When her lips throbbed down below they had a mind of their own and she was not going to ignore its cravings. She actually did not mind giving him any seeing all that he had been through. Still, her kindness would come with a price and that would be him getting her a not guilty verdict. Feeling herself drift back off to sleep, she bounced up needing to get out and bend some corners before it got too late.

"Hey. Hey Ox, get up," Pandora yelled as she crawled over to the side of the bed, shoving Oxy in the head.

"Huh...wha?" Oxy grumbled.

"Get up bitch. You can sleep when you're dead. We got work to do so get dressed."

Chapter 10: "Tell me something I don't know." — Lexi

Diamond shuffled around to the side of the house hoping to be able to hear the noises within. The windows were all shut but she knew from past experiences that neither he nor those cackling bitches of his could keep quiet at any hour but the sleeping one. She moved slowly as not to alert the ones inside but she had to admit for it to be early in the day there was not one sound coming from the house. Usually his minions are rotating the house, cooking and cleaning and making sure everything was in order for when Tino woke up. But on this day the house sounded as if it was lifeless.

She was about to cease her snooping until she heard faint voices in the backyard. Moving quickly yet as quiet as a ninja she headed for the back area hoping to not only get a glimpse of who was back there but also over hear the conversation. Her body pressed against the wall of the house like moss as she slowed her breathing and prayed no one saw her over there, even with the sun casting all sorts of shadow.

"Yeah nigga, you got these bitches on lock don't you?" A heavyset guy addressed Tino as he puffed on his cigar.

"Man these hoes ain't worth a damn. They just looking to get somethin' for nothin' you understand what I'm saying," Tino responded as the men laughed, "Shit they're gonna have to be gone and find themselves somewhere else to live, a nigga getting' too old for this shit."

"Awe man you straight trippin, but you don't look too good though, nigga, you straight?"

"Man, its nothin'. I just need to take my ass to the doctor and get this cold in order you feel me."

"Right, right, aye, so whatever happened to that dark haired bitch you used to fuck with? I would've loved to have that walking around my crib butt hole ass naked baby," the man's belly chuckled as Diamond brought her eye slickly around the corner.

"Man that bitch dead yo, straight up."

"Fuck you mean dead, nigga? You axed the bitch, Tino?"

"Man, she had to be dealt with, caught her stealing. She wasn't nothing but another little crack head hoe, just like the rest of them. She wasn't special," Tino said as he coughed up blood into his handbag, which was already full of it.

"Word, damn that's fucked up, I was really feeling her man. She was right, thick in the waist and she didn't have any stretch marks on her stomach or her titties," The man bowed his head as if he was doing it as a moment of silence for her.

Diamond's disgust grew for Tino as she stood there listening to him lie about her. She was far from a crack head and even though there was a little truth behind her being a whore she most certainly carried herself with class. She did not get with men who did not have money and could not provide for her the miniscule luxuries she was used to. In her eyes, that made it all better. The men seemed to be wrapping up their conversation and heading inside. Diamond reached behind her back pulling out Kojack's gun securing it in her hand.

"Don't move motherfucka!" Diamond yelled crossly, pointing the gun straight ahead.

As she looked around at the air she was pointing towards she realized that she had jumped out a second too late. She wanted to wait until the big dude went into the house before she cornered him but as the cold air slapped her face she quickly understood that her plan was not as well thought out as it seemed in her head. Feeling a bit of defeat and exhausted from all of her planning and coming up short, she tiptoed back to the car trying not to be seen.

"Shit!" she screamed loud and wildly in the car, "Why the fuck?"

Her fingers started the car almost immediately as if her mind unconsciously knew that she could not wait to get out of there. Beyond infuriated and exhausted from failure and lack of sleep, she slowly pulled off wishing she had set a bomb underneath his house so she could watch it explode. The metal of the gun pierced her back while she sat in the seat prompting her to toss it in the glove compartment in a forceful manner. She took one last look at his house deciding that the best time to deal with Tino was when he least expected it, in his bed.

****

Kojack walked through the double automatic sliding glass doors of the hospital heading straight for the information desk. Diamond had not given him any knowledge on how to get to her room, just expecting him to show up and magically get there. Annoyed, he tapped his finger on his cell to call her and retrieve the information she should have given him beforehand.

"How the fuck are you going to tell me to get up here and see about her when you didn't even bother to give me the room or floor number?" he bellowed tossing his hand in his pocket to keep his composure.

"Hey! Don't fucking start with me, alright! I've had a bad fucking morning. Tell Lexi I had to go home because now I don't feel well."

"Fuck all that. What room is she in?" he yelled once more.

"236! 236! Sheesh!" Diamond screamed as she hung up the phone, launching it across the car.

Kojack stood there looking down at his phone for a minute before realizing that he was hung up on. He hated for that to happen to him even though he has dished it out on more than one occasion. He darted for the elevators and waited for his turn to load as the crowd moved slowly inside one of them. It was as if the elevator moved like the speed of lightning as Kojack exited once it reached the second floor.

He headed down the hall weaving through the heavy traffic of doctors, patients, and nurses searching the door plates for room 236. His eyes glanced over a plate that was partially covered by a doctor and a nurse standing in front of it as they gazed down at a chart. Kojack felt he was in the right place and as they moved walking inside the room his feelings were confirmed. He wanted to walk in but part of him needed to brace hisself for whatever it was he was about to see.

"Ms. Burden, how are you feeling?"

He heard the dark skinned doctor speak while adjusting his glasses.

"A little better," Lexi responded groggily giving Kojack the notion that her illness was not life threatening.

"Well I've got your test results back here and I would like to talk to you about a few things," The doctor rambled in his thick African accent while he fumbled through papers.

The pale thin Caucasian nurse stood there beside the doctor ready to assist him when needed. A shadow being cast over by the door broke her concentration on the doctor, taking a look in Kojack's direction. He stood there unable to move as she walked towards him looking like she was about to scold him to death.

"Sir, can I help you?" she asked with her angry eyes meeting him before she did.

"Uh, I'm here to see Lexi," he responded.

"Oh. Come on in. We were just briefing her about her results. Now if she doesn't want you in here you're gonna have to step out for a minute. Okay, Hun?"

Kojack nodded in agreement as she led him into the room. Turning the corner slightly, he gawked down upon Lexi wearing a hospital robe, lying back against the pillow. She had not even taken a look up to see who the nurse invited into the room. The nurse reached over, touching Lexi on the shoulder alerting her to Kojack's presence as the doctor continued to fumble through his medical chart.

"Hun, this young man is here to see you," The nurse whispered while pointing in Kojack's path.

"Hey, Lex," Kojack waved smiling as if he was actually happy to be there.

"Hey," Lexi responded half-heartedly.

"Okay…" The doctor began noticing the tension in the air, deciding to slice through it before he was unable to get his speech out. "Ms. Burden. You really need to slow down on the alcohol and drug abuse. Your system was full of miscellaneous drugs and for a young girl that is most definitely not a good thing."

"Tell me something I don't know," Lexi said placing her head in her hands wondering why the hell Kojack was there.

"You are perfectly healthy, other than that and you are disease free," The doctor continued pretending to ignore her smart remark. "Your pain was just really bad gas."

"Again tell me something I don't know," Lexi smacked her lips with attitude even though she was elated to know that she was AIDS and HIV free.

Her hair was a mess and she bore no makeup, which pissed her off to the fullest. She had never before been caught dead looking anything other than perfect in front of him, even in the early morning. So the fact that she looked like shit drove her insane. Gently and inconspicuously she tried to comb her short bob down a little with her fingers but no matter how she looked she could not bring herself to look up into his eyes. Kojack stood there a bit relieved that he was there to listen to the results of Lexi's tests. He was happy that he did not have to fight with her to get one done.

"Fine. Here's something you don't know, you're pregnant. Congratulations. Oh and you were dehydrated as well. You might want to cut back on all things unhealthy and start thinking about the health of your unborn child. You also might need to call your parents and let them know that you're here," The doctor frowned signaling the nurse as they headed for the door.

"Wait! Wait. I'm sorry I didn't mean to get nasty with you before. This is just all so overwhelming right now. Can you tell me how far along I am?" Lexi asked turning her attention to the shocked look spreading on Kojack's face.

"About 6 weeks Hun. I'll give you some time and I'll be back in a little while," The doctor smiled as he and the nurse left the room.

"6 weeks? Damn. Well, congratulations. That's great for you," Kojack spat nonchalantly.

"Yeah, congratulations to you too motherfucka, because it's yours," Lexi said rolling her neck and eyes simultaneously.

"Mine? How do you know that for sure, girl? Shit, you know how you get down."

"Are you serious right now, Kojack? You are the only nigga that has hit this pussy in the last year so you've got me fucked up. I was fucking with bitches before I met you."

"Man, how do I know that? You could be

still playing games like you've been doing," Kojack thumbed his nose as the words flew from his mouth but a part of him felt stupid for questioning her.

"Is that why you came up here, to fuck with me? I know Diamond pawned me off on you but you didn't have to come, you know. All you know how to do is run the fuck away. So here's your chance. Run."

"Man you gonna stop talking to me like I ain't grown or something—"

"It will always be the age difference with you, isn't it? You just can't allow your fucking heart to love me," Lexi shook her head in disappointment, "And what's fucked up is I can't help but to love you and now I'm pregnant...GET OUT!"

Lexi's voice released an unspeakable torrent that he had never heard come from her lips. Her eyebrows were curled all the way over and she appeared to be breathing much like an angry bull, all that was missing was the smoke from her nose. She pointed to the room door just in case he did not hear her the first time, hoping he just got the drift and left. Her heart could not bear to look at his worthless ass any longer and she needed to mentally prepare to take care of her baby on her own.

"Lexi, I'm...I'm..."

"Sorry? Of course you're sorry. Sorry motherfuckas are always sorry. I can't believe I was stupid enough to believe you could ever love me especially after knowing how you ended it with Pandora. But that was me, being young and dumb and this is me being on some grown woman shit. Get the fuck outta my room and never come back."

"Lex..."

"Diamond should be getting us an apartment soon and then you will have your fucking place back but for right now, I don't want to know you exist," Lexi crossed her arms and turned her head waiting for him to leave the room.

Kojack looked at her expression knowing that she was not playing and astonished by her sudden change in attitude towards him. He had to admit it was quite the turn on to see her so in control of her life. The very thought of her raising a kid that could potentially be his on her own flashed in his head. It was a thought he was not prepared to extinguish or live with. She was going to have to listen to him one way or the other because he refused to be absent from his kid's life.

"I'll leave but this ain't over girl. We need to

talk."

"Nigga get the fuck outta my room!"

Chapter 11: "*My wrath.*" — *Pandora*

"Excuse me, ma'am. I'm sorry but you can't go up there," The doorman said stopping Pandora at the door.

"Well why not it's my condo?"

"Because, ma'am. As of this morning, the property manager has been issued a warrant to seize all of your personal assets including your home. The police are not allowing anyone in your door," The doorman tightened his lips in dismay, "Sorry."

"Argh!" Pandora shouted in rage as she headed back out of the revolving lobby doors.

She walked back out the door meeting Oxy who was patiently waiting on the corner. The two walked off headed back down to the Harrison Street Red Line el station quickly scurrying down the stairs. They remained silent until Oxy became bored with their little rendezvous and began whistling to pass the time away.

"What the fuck is that noise?" Pandora snapped.

"Uh, duh, it's called whistling," Oxy snarled back at her.

"Well stop it. It's giving me a headache."

"Yeah, cause the train station ain't loud enough," Oxy rolled her eyes, "Why are we downtown anyway? I hate it down here. It's always so crowded and motherfuckas is rude."

"Look, if you gonna be with me then stop questioning every little thing I do. That place we just came from used to be my fucking place. I can't believe it's gone."

"Girl, fuck that place. As soon as we're married you'll be in the biggest house we can afford," Oxy smiled, dreaming.

"Yeah, that sounds nice," Pandora did not sound interested at all.

"Why do you always gotta be negative, P? I'm pouring my heart on the table here and you just keep shutting me down."

"Ugh! Shut the fuck up with that sentimental shit, Ox. Damn," Pandora said irritated by her very presence.

"What happened to your spot, Pandora?"

"Does it matter? I lost it okay, along with everything else," Pandora lowered her head thinking how easy life would be if she were dead.

The more she thought about the turn her life has taken all in a couple of months, the more she began to wonder what death would be like. Her soul yearned for a good clean death, one that would not hurt at all and one that she would never see coming. It would be the sweetest taboo for her even though she had not been able to do any of things she wanted to do in life. It all seemed like a distant thought as she mentally prepared for a sweet death much like the one Shakespeare used to describe.

"Is that why you keep threatening Diamond to give you that money? I told you I can give you everything you need baby and more."

"You know, I don't remember agreeing to let you in my business, Ox," Pandora stuffed her hands in her jacket pockets for warmth from the Downtown Chicago tunnel air and walked up to the approaching train's door.

"Hey, if we gonna be together you might as well confide in somebody. What the fuck else are we gonna do?" Oxy smiled devilishly.

Pandora side eyed her not wanting to trust her with any information for one minute. There was something about her that never sat quite right with Pandora from the first moment she began talking to her back in county but the more she talked to her the more she realized that she needed to use her for resources. The train was virtually empty for a middle of the day ride but it made Pandora less edgy. After her arrest, she had always felt like someone was watching her in the shadows.

"I told you everything, so try to get it when I tell you this time. First of all let's get one thing straight. Those bitches stole my money...mine. I would've been able to bail out and afford my own damn lawyer if it weren't for that and now I want my shit back." Pandora spat sternly. "I don't understand why I got to keep explaining this shit to you. It's like you're not listening or something."

"At any cost huh?"

"You damn right at any cost. Those hoes weren't thinking about me so why the fuck should I let this shit go?" The veins in her forehead began to pop out from her torrent.

"Yeah, yeah, I hear ya. I'm just saying niggas get shot for less and you just won't let the shit ride," Oxy retorted, "Over some money?"

"Listen bitch. If I find out you talking to them and telling them shit I swear to Christ you will regret it."

"Pandora, why would I talk to them? I'm not fucking them, I'm fucking you," Oxy reassured her. "Meanwhile I would like to get a bit of that. Shit, I'm fucking frustrated."

"Yeah, well, you and me both," Pandora mumbled, "Meanwhile, if you were really a friend you'd help me give those bitches exactly what they deserve."

"And what exactly is that my fiancé?"

"My wrath," Pandora replied sinisterly.

"Ah ha ha ha ha!" Oxy chuckled holding her stomach for relief then mocked, "Yeah alright boo. I got you. If you down for this shit I'm with you but know that now that I'm out, I ain't going back, straight up."

Pandora slowly looked at her face confused as to why she would think that for one minute she was going back either. Her laughter was insulting. It pierced through her earlobes and made her stomach boil. Her sarcasm ate at her like a flesh eating disease and tore her open from the inside out. She could not for the life of her figure out why this bitch was taking her for a joke.

"I've tasted blood before, Oxy. This shit is real. It's not a damn game," Pandora snarled through her teeth hoping she got the message.

"Okay, okay. I feel you. So you're a bad ass.

Well, what do we do now bad ass?" Oxy asked crossing her legs, giving Pandora her undivided attention.

"Now I need some money to go cop some heat. That's where you come in."

Oxy was not surprised. She knew eventually Pandora was going to come knocking on her Financial Avenue. She smiled and nodded her head refusing to engage in anymore revenge talk. Pandora sensed tension in the air but brushed it off. She knew that regardless of how Oxy felt she would do anything she told her to do including shoot one of her thieving whoring sisters right between the eyes.

"Well I ain't got any money on me. I have to ask my dad," Oxy said staring straight ahead as a bunch of kids walked through the train cars.

"Then ask your dad." Pandora mocked her as she turned looking out the window.

An hour later they had finally made it back to Oxy's house. Pandora raced to the bedroom and dropped her jacket on the floor. Oxy followed close behind to figure out what the hell she was on. She sauntered up to Pandora's waist dropping to her knees to give her center a kiss through her jeans. Her hands firmly gripped her backside, giving it a good squeeze.

"Let me see your phone again," Pandora said tapping her shoulder and reaching out her hand.

"You gonna call your sisters again?"

"Naw girl, damn. Just give me the damn phone," Pandora waved her hand at her wildly expecting the phone to magically appear in her hand.

Once in her possession, she began trying a million different numbers, typing one after the other into the phone trying to get in touch with her old hood hookups. Oxy sat trying not to stare but she was intrigued to know what Pandora's next move was. It was crazy that everything she wanted to do was more important than having sex with her fiancé. She watched as Pandora talked on the phone like she was running a business. Her confidence was sexy but it meant nothing if she could not enjoy it. Frustrated yet again, Oxy fell back on the bed pouting, yearning for just a small taste.

"Hey. I'm home! Is anyone here?" Ivan yelled as he walked to the dining room table.

"Yeah dad, we're up here," Oxy bellowed back, looking at the clock noticing that he was home rather early today.

"We?" Ivan mumbled as he removed his coat and hat and tossing them across the chair.

"Yes we dad. Did you forget that Pandora was here?" Oxy said coming from the staircase while she fidgeted with her fingers.

"With us?" Ivan roared.

"Shhh, dad, lower your voice. She could hear you. I thought you wanted her here. What's the deal?" Oxy stressed.

"Oxy, I do not like that girl. She is bad news and I don't know what you have brought in our house but I don't like it," Ivan was firm sending off a treacherous look unknown to his daughter.

"Shit, it can't be any worse than what's already here."

"What did you just say to me?" Ivan's eyes punctured through Oxy's soul like a piercing gun.

Oxy swallowed the lump that sat in the back of her throat as her heart rate tripled in under a second. Sweat droplets began to form on the smalls of her hands and the back of her ears realizing that she had fucked up. Her only thoughts were that he would save his torment for another time seeing as though they had guests who he surely would not want witnessing what kind of man Ivan really was.

"Dad I..."

"Is everything okay?" Pandora asked as she trotted slowly down the stairs aware that she was interrupting something very heated.

"Yes," Ivan cleared his throat. "Everything's fine Pandora. I was just telling Oxy here that uh, we need to go over your case some more."

"Oh that would be good. Maybe we could do that tonight," Pandora replied before winking and heading back up stairs.

"I'm sorry daddy. I didn't mean to disrespect you," Oxy stated hurriedly bowing her head, "But can I please have some money."

"Money for what Oxy, drugs?"

"No daddy. I...I don't think I want to do drugs anymore," Oxy said calmly as she looked up into her father's astonished eyes. "I just need some money okay? Can you give me some?"

Ivan was shocked by her sudden change of heart. Her eyes were not discolored and her voice resounded with sincerity. He looked down upon her attempting to cast a dark shadow over her frail form. His fist balled up tightly but his arm could not bring itself to raise feeling as though for once in her life she was attempting to follow the rules and obey. Even though he did not want to admit it right then and there his heart was pleased with her sudden change in demeanor.

"Um, well how much do you need, Ox?"

"About $500, but it's just for shopping daddy. So don't worry."

"Just shopping huh?" Ivan side eyed her as he took out his wallet, counting the cash he had inside. "Well I've got four here."

"Perfect. Thanks sir!" Oxy snatched the money from his hand quickly before he was able to change his mind.

"But you know this is going to come with a price don't you?"

"Yes…" she said looking up into his awaiting eyes knowing he was waiting for a better response. "Yes daddy."

"That's better."

Ivan handed her the money and watched closely as Oxy turned and headed upstairs to give Pandora what she desired. When she arrived, she found Pandora hunched over on the bed deep in conversation with someone on her cell. Pandora finally looked up and noticed her in the room rummaging in her closet for a new outfit to wear tonight; she quickly ended the call letting the person know she would call them back when she was ready.

"Guess what girl. I got the money!" Oxy danced as she waved a fan of cash in her hand.

"Straight up, cool, how much is that?" Pandora smiled impressed by her achievement.

"$400!"

"Huh? That's it? Okay boo that's not enough," Pandora laughed.

"Damn, how much you need? Shit I had to beg my dad for this," Oxy barked as she slapped the money down on the dresser like it was worthless.

"Hmm, don't worry about it. You did good babe, but I'll get the money myself. Hey, do you wanna get high?" Pandora asked enthusiastically.

"Oh...uh, naw, I'm good."

"Come on. I know you have something lying around here girl. I don't want to go out tonight sober. Let's get fucked up really quickly. If we do it now we won't be so high that we can't drink later," Pandora insisted.

"Naw girl I'm good on that. I don't wanna

do drugs anymore. Figure I'd turn over a new leaf for my newfound family."

"Wow, well when did you decide that?"

"Today, I realize I don't need that shit you know. The only drug I need is right here baby," Oxy smirked walking up close to Pandora gently rubbing her hand on the front of her jeans then moving slowly in between her legs.

"Awe that's good, I'm proud of you," Pandora recited cynically, "So let's get it in one last time. I mean even though you quit doesn't mean I have to and I've been locked up for weeks sober as hell. I could use something to take the edge off."

"Shit you need something to take the edge off, as uptight as you've been around here. But give me fifteen minutes with my tongue on that clit and I can handle that for you babe."

"No!" Pandora caught her excitement and lowered her voice, "I need to get wasted. You'll give me what I want right?"

Oxy was not big on peer pressure but felt like she could treat herself just one last time to a goodbye high. All of Pandora's talk of getting high just put the thought back in her head of the feeling that she would be missing once she finally gave it all up. She decided that one for the road would not be so bad and that it would be only that one and tomorrow would be a brand new day for her.

"Okay chick. Just one and then we get dressed," Oxy agreed as Pandora jumped up and down for joy.

"That's wassup! So what you got?"

"All I got is these last few Yompers left here. There's like four left in this baggie," Oxy replied as she reached in a porcelain cow head on her dresser and pulled out a small clear baggie with four purple pills inside.

"Cool. Let's get fucked up then!"

Pandora snatched the baggie and took a pill out handing Oxy hers first. Oxy tossed it in her mouth like she was popping Tic Tacs back then swayed her hips around the room waiting for the effects of the pill to take place. Pandora saw that she was more in tune with her high than anything and knew she had her gone.

"Hey, take another one. Two for you and two for me, right? I'm about to go downstairs and grab some apple juice. You want some?" Pandora asked.

"Nope, I'm so good!" Oxy replied as Pandora exited the room without waiting for her response.

Pandora made her way downstairs to retrieve her version of apple juice, which was really cognac in a glass and made it back upstairs to the room in a flash. She found Oxy sitting on the bed rubbing her cheek against her silky smooth comforter engrossed in the feel and texture of it. It was as if she was trying to become one with it, loving the way it danced across her face and made her feel as light as water.

"What are you doing?" Pandora asked with a raised eyebrow.

"Have you ever just felt this blanket? I love it so, so much, you know," Oxy smiled back. "What you got there?"

"Oh this, remember I told you I was going to get some apple juice," Pandora promoted, "You want some?"

Pandora handed the glass in the most tempting gesture to Oxy moving in closer and closer. Oxy took it without hesitation and downed the contents eagerly. She doubled back with a nasty face after she had swallowed the last bit and realized that was no apple juice. Her throat was on fire and her tongue was tingling as she breathed like she was performing Lamaze, holding her neck as if that would cool it off.

"Bitch I think that apple juice was spoiled or something, straight up," Oxy said between breaths.

"What? You never tasted this kind before?" Pandora grinned.

"Naw, never, what kind is that?"

"The cognac kind from your dad's liquor cabinet downstairs," Pandora cackled, "I thought you knew what I meant by apple juice. That's just my little pet name for it just in case someone is listening who ain't supposed to be."

"Oh my God Pandora, I never drank that shit before with these fucking Yompers yo!" Oxy panicked falling to the floor then getting up and plopping down back onto the bed.

"Hmm, how do you like that, a drug addict who doesn't drink when she drives...fascinating."

"Oh my God Pandora! Oh my God!"

"Listen just lay back and calm down. It's okay. All you need to do is sleep it off honey bunny. Get some rest baby and I'll take care of you," Pandora coached evilly.

Oxy lay back on her favorite Hello Kitty pillow, snuggling it like a young toddler. Pandora tucked her into her pink comforter and made sure she was nice and snug before dipping into her closet to check out what kind of clothes she had that would bare all that she needed them to. She came across a beautiful pink and black lace mini dress that fit her body nice and snug like a driving glove. She paired it with a pair of black Jimmy Choo suede strappy sandals and tasseled her hair out of its ponytail as she headed out the bedroom door. Her eyes peeled back for a brief second to make sure Oxy was spread out undisturbed. Once she saw Oxy drooling on the pillow she knew she was down for the count.

Pandora waltzed down the stairs tucking the little baggie with the remaining two Yompers away in her bra as she looked out the windows noticing that the sun was at its highest of the day signaling a time of around 3pm. It was beginning to creep back down the sky prompting nightfall to take place but before it did she had work to do. Downstairs she found Ivan sitting at the dining room table slumped over in a chair with papers in front of him on the table. He had his usual cocktail sitting next to the half-drunk bottle and a smidgen of snoring sounds could be heard emanating from his nose. She used that quiet time to unleash her plan. Removing one of the pills from the baggie in her bra, she bit into it to make it easier for the rest of it to crumble as she pressed with her hands sending the pieces of it plummeting into his drink.

"Mmm," Ivan stirred, rising groggily, "What are you doing?"

"Nothing, I just came to talk to you about the case, like you requested," Pandora jumped back, "Shouldn't we go into your office?"

"Uh, no, we can do it right here."

"Okay well where do we begin?" she licked her lips pushing his glass out of the way of the papers.

"Hold on now. Don't ever mess with a man and his drink," Ivan said taking the drink from her reach then taking a nice deep sip from it.

"Well, excuse me. I thought I would just get a better look at these papers," Pandora lied, "Honestly, I thought I might take a sip or two."

"Oh no you won't," Ivan snapped as she rubbed his hairy arm soothingly.

Ivan removed his arm quickly not liking her touch. In his eyes, she was poison from her soft skin to her angelic looking eyes. Her body was that of a slithering Medusa tail and she gave off the persona of a deadly Black Widow spider. She was bad for business and he was determined to steer clear of everything about her. Besides, he had everything he needed right in his own home and now that it was back, safe and sound with him, he knew what he had to do to keep it right where it belonged. He took another sip from his glass and then a big gulp finishing its contents and pouring his self another glass never taking his eye off of her for a second.

"Let's get one thing straight here darling. I don't trust ya. Okay? I think you're a snake in the grass and you...you probably did kill that guy on purpose. He didn't disrespect you or your sisters, did he? Naw, I know he didn't," Ivan's words were beginning to slur.

"NO! That son of a bitch deserved everything that he had coming and I don't give a shit who doesn't believe me. He was a waste of perfectly good space and now that he's gone I feel no fucking remorse," Pandora argued angrily making sure to get close to his face to stress her point.

"You are bad..." Ivan slurred as he sat back in his seat staring up at the ceiling fan watching it twirl around in its rapid motion.

"What's that daddy?" Pandora walked around standing behind him running her fingertips down his chest in a seductive manner.

"You're a cold blooded...murderer," Ivan began to shake his head profusely trying to shake off the dizzy, warm feeling circling his head.

"Oh am I? Are you sure about that counselor?" Pandora leaned down to nibble on his ear.

Ivan felt like he could not move, like there was a colossal sized boulder holding him down. Her tongue manipulated his nerves sending tingling sensations down to his loins, loins that had not been sparked in years, not since his muse left him. He could not for the life of him figure out why he was allowing her to get him excited; especially when he despised someone like her. But at that moment she made him feel like he was a king in his own castle. He released a long drawn out breath before succumbing to her advances. As soon as he did that she knew she had him locked. She hopped her small frame up on top of the table in front of him, scooting the papers back behind her and spreading her legs open hiking her skirt up above her thick brown thighs to give him a good visual.

Ivan's senses were heightened and they only rose higher once he feasted his eyes on her loveliness. He pressed on fighting the urge to pass out but the sweet scent of vanilla was calling him and he needed to find it, taste it. He leaned forward in search of the sweet, tangy smell that enveloped his being and smacked his lips together feeling as though he could even taste it already. Pandora smiled, as she knew exactly what he was going through. She put her finger up to his lips teasing him erotically then forced him to lick the remaining crushed Yomper residue off at the same time.

"How does that taste?" she asked in a deep yet womanly voice, leaning back feeling the warmth of his breath against her right thigh.

"Mmmm," Ivan muttered stretching out his tongue as the tip of it caught a small single taste.

Pandora mushed his head into her lace thong giving him a nudge into the right direction, "Taste it, daddy."

Ivan could no longer fight the watering in his mouth as he used his teeth to maneuver her thong to the left side of her v-like opening then stuffed his nose into its gushiness. He moved his face in a circular motion giving her a bit of a tease before opening his mouth and unleashing his tongue to taste the fruits of her nature. It was the most delectable thing he had ever had in his mouth. No other pussy in his life had compared to the sweet nectar that he was sucking from right then. It was tantalizing and mesmerizing, as he grabbed her waist pulling it towards him desiring more. Pandora exhaled rolling her hips to the motions of his head pressing his head further and further into her pussy.

"Nice baby. Just like that. Let me feel that stubble on your chin fuck my pussy baby," Pandora moaned sounding as though she was an experienced porn star.

Ivan felt his manhood stand at attention, reaching his hand down in his pants to give it a good stroke. It was stone cold hard as if he had taken three Viagra pills back to back. Pandora leaned forward looking down at his hard work, smashing his face further into her hoping to smother him. Ivan jerked back trying to breathe but the harder he did the more she pushed. For a small woman, she was definitely very strong. He jerked up hard causing him to back out of her pussy, pushing the chair away from him as he stood.

"I'm gonna show you how to be bad," Ivan breathed heavily as he pulled her legs to bring her ass cheeks closer to the edge of the table.

"Agh!" Pandora exhaled as he pulled her forcefully.

Ivan ripped her thong clean off of her pussy like it was toilet paper. Pandora was astonished by his level of strength looking up into his eyes to see where his head was. His other head, however, was on its way inside of her and if it were not for its colossal size she would not have noticed its presence on her pussy. She looked down to witness the beating she was about to endure but was interrupted by Ivan's body leaning against hers. He laid his head on her shoulder becoming immersed in her gushy tight wet pussy.

Pandora put her chin on his shoulder gripping his slightly muscular build feeling the strength in his thrust as he made his way deeper and deeper inside of her. Her body began to shake with every plunge he took as she closed her eyes trying to concentrate on the pain and pleasure. Ivan began to moan heavily as he pulled out then rammed back in the tight, wetness that enveloped him invitingly. He wrapped his arms around her waist so that she could not weasel her way away from him. She felt her mouth open slightly while moaning flowed uncontrollably. The power behind his log was much more than she could bear as he rammed deeper hoping to make her cry even a little bit for not knowing what she was dealing with.

Her eyes teared up but she refused to let them fall as her head jerked up and down from his motions. Ivan squeezed his fingertips massaging her back in a rough style while his waist jerked repeatedly and his right leg shook in a James

Brown motion. He could feel cum rising inside of him but was resistant to letting it free. It was too early for it to burst so rather than seem like he was incapable of banging her back out he focused on keeping form and thought about running long distant races. With her eyes closed, Pandora looked up staring at the shining light pressed against the wall.

In the mist of it and with her mouth agape from being stuck in sex face, she peered out at a shadow creeping up the stairs. Initially she had no clue of what it could be but she had a good feeling. Busy with the feeling penetrating her pussy like a power drill, she decided not to focus on it too much. But then staring back at her on the steps was Oxy in total shock and unable to tear her eyes away from the horrific scene before her. They locked eyes tightly and as Pandora breathed deeply from Ivan's work. She slowly formed a sinister looking smile on her face and began laughing, while Oxy stood immobile then disappeared.

Chapter 12: "And if my name is Diamond, then what?" — Diamond

Daylight savings time got the best of Diamond as the night sky appeared more rapidly than she had anticipated. She looked down at her cell phone checking the time and realizing that it was definitely late in the evening and she needed to head back to Tino's house. She needed to keep watch of who went in and out of the house for the next few hours so when she infiltrated she would not be caught off guard as to who was in the house with her. She mapped out her plan all day in her head ready to snap the necks of his minion's first then plug a few in his body before making him beg for his life. In her mind, it looked awesome. It was pictured as something out of an old mobster's movie. She had always dreamed of being a bad bitch in that nature and now she had her chance.

She hopped out of the car and headed inside of the BP gas station just up the street from Tino's suburban home. It was a very large one with almost twenty tanks and at almost eight o'clock at night the place was damn near empty. Diamond entered the store looking around spotting a few snacks she could nipple on in the car while she waited for her target dead time, 3 am. She snagged a family size bag of regular flavored Doritos, two bottles of flavored water and three bags of skittles. The sugar was to keep her awake and alert for all those hours.

Her feet ached in her all black Air Force ones and her jeans felt too tight around her waist even though they really were not. The lack of rest and the level of stress she had endured over the past few weeks, had begun to take its toll on her, not giving any consideration to the health of her body. She found herself becoming weaker and weaker by the day so her now or never was this day. Tino's death had to come sooner than later because she might not be strong enough soon to enact her revenge, especially with the life inside of her draining her of every nutrient she put inside of her body. Diamond stood in the line with two people ahead of her, irritated by the lack of experience and speed the cashier displayed.

"What do ya got there?" The cashier joked as she finally made her way to the counter plopping her full arms of junk food down on top of it.

"A bunch of shit, now ring me up," Diamond snarled at him looking around at the million and one things on the counter trying to see if she needed to pick up something else.

"Will that be all for you this evening?" The

Arabic man asked scanning the items slowly that she had so nicely thrown on the counter.

"Throw in that Snickers and that Butterfinger, and oh give me some of those Sour Patches right there."

"You want the big bag or the little bag?"

"The big bag motherfucka, damn. I pointed to those," Diamond laughed pointing to the biggest bag of candy over the man's shoulder.

"Okay, okay. Don't get your t-shirt in a bunch. I'm just trying to help you. That is all," the cashier said as he whisked a bag out from under his counter and passed it to her, "$11.35."

"Damn, I didn't even get shit and you talking about some $11.35 nigga. Is you serious right now?" Diamond's faced curled in disbelief, "Damn y'all straight rapin' niggas and shit."

The man was silent as she slapped a fifty-dollar bill on the counter and bagged her own groceries. She checked out the short stocky woman behind her who was ogling her hard as ever. Diamond was never one to discourage someone from admiring her timeless beauty but she was not in the best of mood. Her eyes cut back at the fair skinned Caucasian woman then back at the cashier as she finished bagging her items.

"Here's your change Hun," the cashier said handing the money to her.

"Uh, naw, just keep it and put it on pump six," Diamond replied waving the man off as she headed for the door.

A part of her wanted to turn to keep going and forget about the lady. On the other hand, she wanted to go back and ask that bitch what her problem was. Instead she continued on to her car attempting to blow off the strange encounter while popping open the bag of Sour Patches she had just paid for.

"Hey! Excuse me!" A voice called from the distance as she approached the back of the car.

She popped the gas door open then twisted the gas cap off without skipping a beat on popping the tiny sugar covered gummy bears in her mouth. Diamond was not even paying attention to her surroundings seeing as though in the hood there were always people around yelling obscenities, so it felt natural to her. She struggled to place the bag of food on the trunk of the car while still maintaining the open bag of candy as she reached for the gas pump. It slowly began to dawn on her that if she followed through with Lexi's plan to carry the baby to full term that she would undoubtedly become a fat pile of lard in no time, scrimmaging for left overs at the bottom of the refrigerator.

"Bitch I said HEY!" The stocky woman delivered a hefty slap to Diamond's mouth knocking the bag of candy out of her hand and onto the ground.

"What the fuck? Bitch, are you serious right now? Have you lost your fucking mind?" Diamond was startled by the slap though it did not deter her from bending down to pick up the remainder of the candy still left inside of the bag.

"Naw, I'm not crazy. Your name is Diamond. Isn't it?" The lady's breath pounded the air.

The woman's dark hair fluttered from underneath her thin black cap and her makeup looked as if it were running down her face for days. She was dressed in her pajamas wrapped in a thick brown leather jacket with fur running across the top. Her feet adorned a fresh pair of Air Max's, which proved to be very sturdy on the slippery slushy snow.

"And if my name is Diamond, then what?"

"Then this!" The woman delivered another hefty blow to her face and even though Diamond was able to combat that one this time she failed to hold onto her bag of candy once more.

"Bitch I swear if you put your hands on me one more time it's gonna be me and you in these streets," Diamond warned as she picked up the candy with even fewer pieces inside this time. "Now you look like an older bitch and I respect my elders and shit but you are testing me and that's gonna get your ass tagged."

"You want to talk about tagging asses? Huh? Well how about my husband's ass that you've been tagging for some years now. Huh? Talk about that ass!" The woman charged at her again.

"Slow down with your crazy ass!" Diamond yelled as she pushed her back.

"No! No, I will not slow down. You and my husband have been having this glorious affair with him coming home smelling like you and money missing from our bank accounts and then it hit me…" The woman paused to catch her breath, bouncing up and down like a pro boxer with her dukes in the air. "Hire a private investigator."

"What the fuck? Hoe, I don't even know your man."

"Oh I think you know him very well. See I got pictures of you and him together. I know the hotels he takes you to and I know the car he rents just to pick you up," The woman continued with tears flowing down her golden frosted cheeks.

"Rented?"

"Yes rented."

"Uh…uh, 'cause, see all of the niggas who I fucked with is paid okay. None of my niggas ride in shit that ain't theirs."

"How would you know? Did you check his registration for the motherfucka?" The woman chuckled. "You simple bitches are all the same, always looking for a handout when you should be looking for a damn job. Well I've got one picture you might be interested in seeing."

"Naw, I'm done with you," Diamond turned around trying to ignore the lady sticking the pump in her car and pulling the latch so the gas would pump itself.

"Oh but I think you aren't just yet, Ms. Diamond. See because you weren't the only one my husband was screwing around on me with behind my back," she pulled a medium sized photograph from her inside pocket and handed it to her, "Tell me what you see, Ms. Diamond."

"Naw, I ain't looking at that," Diamond

refused pushing away the picture and popping another Sour Patch in her mouth.

"Look at the damn picture, bitch!"

Diamond gazed into the woman's eyes veering through pain and anguish before snatching the photo out of her hands. She was not in the mood for anymore of her meaningless efforts to confront her and was ready to get back on her mission. Feeling as though it was the only way to get rid of her she peered down at the black and white photo and could not believe her eyes.

"Sergeant Sutter's," Diamond gasped covering her mouth partially as candy particles flew from her mouth, "What's he doing?"

"He's kissing a man in the bushes at Marquette Park bitch. Yeah that's right your beloved moneybags and my husband are on the down low. He is fucking gay!"

"Oh my God, and I sucked his..." Diamond knew it was not the place to finish her sentence or she feared another ass whooping.

"Well he's been doing this for years. So you should probably go check out your pussy bitch 'cause he's got full blown AIDS," The woman said calmly as if she did not want anyone else to hear what she was saying. "And I've got it too."

"Oh my God!" Diamond placed her hand on her stomach feeling nauseated and light headed all at the same time.

"Yeah, so now that I've destroyed your life allow me to go forth unto the world and destroy the lives of the other bitches he's slept with."

"So that means that I've been stalking this nigga for shit?" Diamond whispered to herself, "Did you just find out that you had it?"

"I went to the doc— Wait a minute. You knew you had it. Didn't you?" the woman read Diamond's face like a blind person reading braille.

"What? I don't know what you talking about," Diamond spoke quickly as she unhooked the gas pump from her car shoving it back into its holster than returning the gas cap to her car.

"You knew you had it bitch and you gave it to my man!" the woman screamed at the top of her lungs slapping her in the head with the picture.

She grabbed Diamond's hair pulling it down to her level before beating her in the head with her other fist. The woman made it a point to hold on tight so that she could not wiggle through her fingertips, wrapping the fibers of her hair around them. Diamond swung up hoping to hit the bitch in her face and startle her enough that she would eventually let go but it appeared to be no use. The more she swung the more the woman treated her like a rag doll, flinging her small stature from left to right.

"Help, help, get this big bitch off of me!" Diamond screamed grabbing her hands trying to pry through her fingers, "Somebody!"

"You're gonna die today bitch, today!"

Diamond acted like a wild bull jerking and kicking away. Nothing else mattered but getting away from the woman's strong grasp. Diamond dug her fingers as deep as she could into the woman's arms letting her know that she was not playing anymore games with her. Her nails were dug down so deep that the woman began to scream feeling like Diamond was surely digging for blood. The woman brought Diamond's head all the way down to force it in between her legs and lock her in to pound her back but Diamond was not having it. A weakness was felt within the woman's grasp as though she was getting tired of the whole ordeal giving Diamond an opening. She yanked hard trying to get free but the woman was smarter and surprisingly quicker than that repositioning her weight to keep a hold on Diamond's hair.

"Ay, y'all stop that shit!" A voice yelled.

Chapter 13: "Awe, naw. I'm not trying to kill nobody...yet." — Lexi

"Are you ready to go home, Ms. Burden?" The nurse said smiling and entering the room with a field of papers.

"Yeah, I guess, as ready as I'll ever be," Lexi sighed trying to gather the rest of her belongings and pack them inside of the hospital issued plastic bag.

"Okay now the doctor prescribed some meds for you, which are nothing more than some prenatal pills and iron pills to make the life growing inside of you big and strong," The nurse was overly happy.

It made Lexi very uncomfortable since she was not the least bit happy about being pregnant or being alone. She had envisioned her life being more luxurious than what it was. Her life was supposed to consist of traveling the world with her dream man and begins with him proposing to her under a French moonlight in Paris. She was supposed to be every woman to her man pleasing him not only in his pants but also in his heart and his mind stimulating his mental every chance she got. Her mother was never around to teach her how to love a man but she was definitely going to do her research to ensure she kept hers happy.

"Thanks," she replied uninterestedly.

The more she thought about the life she could have had with Kojack the more it began to sadden her that it would never come to pass; at least not while he was indifferent about where he wanted to be. She knew eventually she would have to let him see his kid but she had a whole eight months left before that was going to happen, which also meant he had eight months to get his shit together as well. In the end, after what he had put her through, she felt they would probably never be in a relationship. She would always be the young girl in his life and he would always find a reason to leave.

"Child, you don't seem happy about being a new mother. This is supposed to be a happy time, a time for celebration." The nurse hyped as she moved in to pinch Lexi's cheeks, something she always despised. "If you don't mind me prying in your business, what's wrong?"

"I really don't want to talk about it, ma'am."

"Hmm, sometimes you youngsters need to talk about your problems. Maybe if more of you talked it out then there would be less killing."

"Awe, naw, I'm not trying to kill nobody...yet."

The women laughed. Lexi felt a sense of ease as she took a deep breath exhaling it. It was the first time since her breakup with Kojack that she had smiled. The nurse sat down on the bed and spanked a portion of it next to her urging Lexi to take a break from packing and take a seat. She wanted to resist but thought it best not to as she needed some motherly advice right then. The nurse looked considerably older even though she did not know her true age, she just took her as someone who was wise in her ways and felt the need to listen to what she had to say.

"That man that came in here earlier; he's the father of my baby," Lexi breathed as she sat down next to her.

"Oh ok, that's an awesome thing. Most of the young moms that come up in here have no clue of who they slept with the night before, let alone who the father of their baby is. So consider yourself lucky."

"But I'm not lucky. He's an ass. He broke up with me, basically on my birthday and he refuses to talk about it. Now all of a sudden my sister tells him I'm in the hospital and he wants to come and see how I'm doing? I don't think so."

"Honey but he came. You are so busy looking at the negative that you can't accentuate the positive. If he didn't care about you he wouldn't have been here and… he wouldn't be standing in the hall waiting for you either."

A broad smile filled the nurse's oval shaped face. She hoped that would make Lexi smile as well and send her racing out the door to find him. Instead Lexi rose from the bed and stood there staring at the door wondering why he was out there. Her breathing sped up as she contemplated her next move. The nurse witnessed her hesitation and rose to block her line of sight to the door.

"See honey, no one can raise a child alone. Now after having a brief conversation with him in the hall, I can see he truly is sorry for whatever it is he's done," The nurse said sweetly as she caressed her shoulder lightly. "Just hear the man out. If it sounds like bullshit you know what to do baby."

"I don't know. This is the second time he's abandoned me knowing how we feel about each other. It's my age and I understand that but the way he's going about it is wrong."

"Your age, girl you're pregnant now? What other harm can be done at this point?" The nurse shrugged, "Truth be told, you need to figure out what you're going to do because raising a baby alone is no joke. You either need its daddy or an abortion."

She walked to the door peeping carefully out of the small rectangular shaped window noticing a nervous Kojack pacing the floor, "You decide."

The nurse toddled out of the door leaving Lexi with her thoughts. There was not much to think about when it came down to Kojack, in her mind. She knew that gut punching him where it hurt was all that would whip him into shape. The one thing in the world she desired, she was denied, so she was not about to be a fool and keep handing him her heart on a platter for him to feast a little then discard the rest. She headed towards the door opening it forcefully, unafraid of facing him.

"Get in here, Kojack," she said heading back towards the bed to finish packing without looking up at him.

"Lexi, I know what you said about leaving you alone but I need to talk to you. We need to talk this out," Kojack walked up to her grabbing the bag from her hands and slamming it down on the bed.

"Don't fucking touch me, I just don't get why you wanna talk to me now. You never wanted to talk before. Cowards don't talk they run.

Remember?"

"Alright I deserve that," Kojack replied massaging his chin, "But things have obviously changed."

"Why, 'cause I'm carrying a baby?" Lexi squinted, folding her arms. "You know I thought about gut punching you and telling you that it wasn't yours but then I said you know what, that's too easy for you. You've had life too easy up 'til now and that's why you always run away from your problems."

"I don't run away, I just need time to think,"

"No, be a man and call it what it is, running!" Lexi rubbed her head for stress relief, "You know what amazes me is that even though I'm only seventeen, I'm more of an adult than you'll ever be."

"I...okay. I can't take this anymore," Kojack said grabbing Lexi's arm pulling her close to him.

SLAP!

"Stop! No!" Lexi pushed and shoved trying to get him off of her.

Kojack let go gently hoping she did not run out the door and scream rape. He was fucked up in the head that his plan backfired realizing at that moment that she was indeed more of an adult than she really is. She is stronger and more level headed than both of her sisters and when she is sober she appears to be on her game one hundred percent. He knew his typical lines and fetching looks were not going to be enough to convince her to take him back; underestimating her intelligence was his first downfall.

"Lex, I'm sorry. I just don't want you to alienate me from your life or the baby's life."

"Just answer me this, was my age that hard for you to accept when you were planting your face in between my legs tasting me? Was your dick worried about my age when I was riding it in the front seat of your car? Or when you were banging me from the back pulling my hair tightly making me squirm?" Lexi ran her fingers across his zipped up black leather jacket.

Her fingers tapped against his jacket yet in his mind they felt like feathers on his chest. It was hard to explain the way she made him feel when she was around him. It was a feeling that no other woman has ever been able to make him feel and that was the number one reason why he left her alone. Kojack knew if he did not jolt out of her grasp he would never be able to leave her and do the right thing in the eyes of the law of Illinois. In that state, sex with a seventeen year old who was considered a minor was illegal but he could not help who he painfully desired. Granted she played games to get him but her game worked and he was definitely hooked, unable to fight the temptation any longer. The fact that she was carrying his baby was icing on the cake.

"Baby, I…"

"Naw, don't baby me. Your ass is worthless. Know that me and you are over, Kojack."

"How you gonna leave me with my seed in your stomach, girl? You ain't got no money and no place to go. Diamond ain't gonna take care of your ass. So you might as well come be with me and quit playing damn it," Kojack advised firmly.

"See your smug ass still can't see past your money. I don't want your stupid, fucking money. I want you to be a damn man, get your shit together and realize that you were an asshole for punishing me for our love."

"I'm not punishing you," Kojack paused turning towards the door," I'm punishing me and you're getting hurt in the process. I'm just having a hard time dealing with this shit, Lex. I mean, have you ever taken a second out to think about me in all of this?"

"Every damn second, I know what could

happen to you if the wrong people found out, but Kojack, did you ever stop to think that no one is going to find out? Did you ever think about the fact that no one cares? I won't be seventeen forever and I for damn sure won't be acting seventeen with a baby."

In actuality, he had not thought about any of her scenarios. She made valid points but all Kojack could think about was the fear of doing hard time in a county jail all in the name of love. She was an amazing person and an even more amazing lay but he struggled with the one question that he could not find an answer to. Was she more than worth it? He did not want the answer to be yes simply because she was carrying his child.

"Can we talk about this back at the house...please?" Kojack winced picking up her light bag throwing it over his shoulder.

"I guess, since I have nowhere else to go."

"I didn't mean that, Lex," Kojack sighed. "Anyway, I figure we could stop and get something to eat and then go to my office so I can get something I left there."

"It's not what you meant, it's what you said. Don't try to change the damn subject, but whatever."

"Have you heard from Diamond yet?" Kojack replied trying to switch the subject to a lighter mood. "Does she know about the baby?"

"About the baby, don't trip on that cause I'm getting an abortion," Lexi retorted as she headed out the hospital room door.

Chapter 14: "Prove it." — Oxy

"This shit was never supposed to happen," Ivan snarled as he backed out of Pandora's snatch relieved of all of his stress.

"But it did. So try to take it back," Pandora teased hopping down off of the table straightening her dress.

"You just keep your mouth shut, alright?" he replied with heavy panting desiring to taste her sweet lips.

"I'll think about it," she smirked as she headed for the staircase, "You just make sure I can beat that case lover."

Ivan knew that he had been played, used and he hated the feeling that followed. He felt dirty, icky, and nasty needing to cleanse his self of all the wrong doing that took place just minutes ago. He rubbed his skin attempting to remove the leftover smell that lingered from her juicy, tasting opening. The more he scrubbed the more the smell spread, refusing to disappear. He turned, watching as she disappeared up the stairs like a quiet little rat as he headed for the kitchen to try and rinse off.

Pandora slowly ventured up to the bed to

check on Oxy. Her eyes were closed and the slight snoring that was present before she left was still sounding off. She appeared as though she had not actually moved since Pandora left. Her shoulders shrugged feeling as though she may have imagined her watching them, even though it felt so erotically real. She lived for shit like that, making other people jealous and pissing people off. To her, it was stupid of Oxy to believe that she would ever marry her. Another woman would never get all of her ever again.

Without slipping out of her party clothes, she slid in on the opposite side of the bed being careful not to stir Oxy as she slid under the thick covers. She relaxed her tired bones staring up at the clock on the wall noticing that it was rather early for her to be in the bed, 7:45 pm. Her eyes could not find a way to drift to sleep regardless as to how soothing Oxy's snoring became. She turned over on her left side staring out the window at the trees blowing in the wind thinking heavily that it was a sign, a sign for her to get the hell out of there before the good Attorney could inevitably decide her fate. Pandora closed her eyes forcing herself to fall asleep from boredom, feeling that when the sun made its presence in the sky again she would put her thoughts in motion.

Two hours went by without movement or

noise in the room. Oxy rose, creeping out the bed effortlessly like she was floating on air, still feeling the effects of the drugs and alcohol she had previously consumed. She stood at the foot of the bed gawking down on Pandora's golden face as she slept unaware that she was being surveyed. Oxy took her fingers running them along the tops of her bare naked toes testing to see if that would stir her but when it never did she knew she was in a dark, deep sleep.

"Is she asleep?" Ivan said peeping slightly in the door.

"Shh," Oxy hurriedly scampered shoving his head back out the door and closing it behind her, "You put the bitch to sleep now you wanna wake her up?"

"No. I was actually coming in there to get you," he replied walking back down the stairs.

"I bet you were," Oxy expressed following right behind him.

"I was. I told you I don't like her."

"You sure have a funny way of showing it. She belonged to me. She was mine and you spoiled her!"

"Lower your fucking voice to me. I am still

your daddy."

"What the fuck ever. Some fucking daddy you are, sleeping with my girlfriend," Oxy fumed shaking her head and crossing her arms. "I thought you would never do that to me?"

"Hey you listen to what the fuck I say! You got that," Ivan reached down wrapping one hand of his strong fingers around her tiny neck, squeezing just enough to send her the message, "She's poison. She seduced me."

"I'm sorry daddy. I just figured since my mom left that you would be all mine. You would never give it to anyone else. I haven't fucked any other men, only bitches and you just took one from me."

"You went rogue, Oxy. You wanted to go out in the streets and act crazy and run with fools while I sat here deprived. After your mom left, you said you would take care of me."

"I know what I said. I just…I just needed a break is all," Oxy lowered her head in shame feeling badly that she had disappointed Ivan, "You said that you would always understand about my needing to spread my wings and fly so long as I didn't fuck other men. Well I'm only fucking women but I will never stop loving you, daddy."

Truth be told, she was torn between the idea of being with her mother's husband and the fact that everyone outside of them considered her his stepdaughter. It felt a bit sickening at times but at others she was in heaven. Her break away from him only heightened the long-lived infatuation she has had for him, since her pussy was old enough to throb. They had been fucking since she was sixteen but now that she was a grown woman and done running the streets and running from his love, she was determined to get the one thing every young girl dreamt about, the ring.

"Well I hope you've sowed enough oats because if you ever leave me again, we are done," Ivan snarled worse than a ferocious dog. "No more lavish hand me outs, no more daddy dick, nothing."

"Oh yeah, well give me a reason to stay if you want me here so badly."

Oxy wrapped her scrawny arms around his neck allowing his tongue to slap box with hers. Her lips had never graced the lips of another man and her pussy belonged to him as well. He was okay with her doing girls because they were not any kind of threat to him. He laid pipe and knew no bitch or dildo could ever amount to that. As he ran his muscular hands down her back to her flat almost nonexistent backside, he began to become aroused ready for round two except with her. As they continued to make out heavily in the hall, she began to become turned off, tasting the very essence of her pussy in his mouth.

"Wait!" Oxy groaned backing away from his advances. "You have to promise me that you will never fuck her again."

"Oxy, I told you that I don't fucking like her."

"Do you take me for some kind of fool? You licked her pussy, daddy. I taste her all in your mouth. You've never licked my pussy before and we've been together for years," Oxy folded her arms pouting like a five year old.

"She made me. I told you she made me."

"Well you're gonna get on your knees and lick mine too, then," Oxy demanded.

"Anything you want me to do, I'll do," Ivan responded feeling hotter than ever for Oxy as he leaned in sucking her neck, moving down to her petite breasts.

"Oh my God!" Oxy paused, "You're in love with her, aren't you?"

"What? No, no you've got it all wrong. How could I love her? I don't even know her."

"You don't love her, daddy?"

"No. I don't," he replied between kisses.

"Prove it."

Ivan halted his lustful act then looked away from her gaping over at the moonlight shining through the window. He rubbed the left over spittle from his lips massaging all the way down to his chin before looking back up into accusing eyes. Oxy reached up scratching her fingers on his chin stubble like he was a helpless puppy. Their history together twinkled in their eyes as they stared deeply, reading each other's thoughts like soul mates.

"Go do it right fucking now," Oxy whispered to his face. "And when you're done, I'm going to take good care of you."

"Yeah…mmmm," Ivan moaned as he leaned in to slob her down once more but was halted by her finger to his lips.

"There will be plenty of time for that later. Right now is business," she demanded.

As Ivan headed for his office, Oxy remained by the stairs looking in the direction of her room trying to see if there was any movement. Oxy danced wondering what the hell was taking him so long then noticed how dark the house actually was. She began to grow impatient swallowing her insecurities about the dark and slowly heading back towards the office. A dark figure emerged prompting her to back up her stride all the way to the mildly lit area of the dining room, watching as Ivan loaded his gun.

"Are you sure you wanna do this cause once it's done there's no going back," Ivan questioned as he finished loading and securing the piece.

"Get your ass up those stairs so we can fuck already," Oxy smiled.

Ivan moved with haste, heading up towards her bedroom with Oxy tugging close behind. She bit her nails but she was far from scared anxious to see what Pandora's brains would look like plastered all over the wall. Thoughts ran through her mind about burying her in the back yard directly under her window so she could think of what they had from time to time and still feel like she was in her life. Remorse for her flew right out the window the closer they came to the bedroom door and anger began to fill her head with the thoughts of Pandora's eyes when Ivan was banging her.

"Hey. Don't get any blood on my Hello Kitty blanket, alright. I really like that blanket."

"Ox, you can buy another blanket," Ivan shrugged.

"So but I like that blanket. Why should I go buy another one when I have one already? Just don't get any fucking blood on it."

"Are you shittin' me right now?"

"No. Ugh, just go," Oxy urged.

Ivan carefully pushed the bedroom door hoping it would not make a squeak. As they tipped in the room their eyes were focused on the big lump on the bed waiting for it to stir as they moved in closer. Oxy placed her hand on Ivan's arm gripping his Oxford button down as tight as could be. He looked back urging her to let him go as he inched around to the side of the bed to peel back the covers and get one last look at the beautiful goddess before he destroyed the wonderful canvas forever. The sound in the room was eerily quiet, not even the sound of breathing could be detected. Ivan fidgeted at the side of the bed looking up at Oxy for reassurance.

"Go on," she mimed using her hands in a shoving gesture.

The fingers on his right hand made a typing motion as he toyed with the notion of killing something so beautiful and then it hit him. He was mildly attracted to her. He could not make out if it was the mind-blowing sex that had him gone or if it was indeed her beauty but something in him could not bear the thought of ending that connection for good.

"Do it!" Oxy encouraged as she walked over to pull back the blanket herself.

She whisked the blanket away from the bed gazing down upon a long formed pile of clothes. The sight of the clothes angered Oxy to the max as she tussled through them screaming at the top of her lungs and searching the room. Ivan grabbed her by the arm forcing her to grab a hold of herself as he quietly pointed towards the closet. He knew she could not have gotten far and the jump from the balcony would have indeed injured her. Besides the sliding glass balcony door was closed, which was something that could not be accomplished from the outside. The closer they got to the closet door the more the anticipation built inside of the two of them.

"Ha, bitch!" Oxy roared as she slid the closet door over and flicking the wall light. "Where the fuck is this bitch?"

Pandora made a quick dash out of the bathroom, which was next to the room exit and high-tailed it down the steps and on towards the front door. Her feet moved swiftly like a roadrunner trying to get away from the two craziest motherfuckas she had ever encountered. Ivan and Oxy were on her ass like white on rice, watching as she struggled with the front door locks.

"Shoot her ass! Don't let her get out!" Oxy screamed shoving Ivan slightly.

Oxy stood waiting on her blood to splatter all over the corridor already thinking about what cleansing product to use to clean it up. She looked at her attire wondering how she had gotten dressed that fast; feeling as though she might not have ever been sleep and was only pretending when she was standing over her. If that were the case it meant Pandora heard every single word they said. Ivan shot shattering one of the door's glass triangles imbedded inside, which was two feet higher than Pandora. Finally the door opened freely, as she ran out in a panic without looking back. Oxy looked over at Ivan evilly knowing exactly what he did.

"Do you expect me to believe that you seriously missed her by accident? You're a fucking ex-army nerd for Christ sakes," Oxy crossed her arms showing the most sinister look on her face. "If you are in love with that bitch then go be with her."

"I don't fucking love her," Ivan swallowed knowing he was only partially telling the truth.

"Then I'm going to get the car and you are going to run around to the back of the house and go after that bitch and this time, don't miss. She will fuck up your career, daddy. She will let everyone know what goes on in this house. She's poison. Remember?" Oxy coaxed, "Do you want her to fuck up your awesome lifestyle and your respectable career?"

"Hell no!"

"Then go get that bitch!" Oxy pointed, "NOW!"

Ivan did not hesitate to follow directions. This was no longer about Oxy it was about him. She was right. He could not allow Pandora to get away and exploit his business to anyone. He could not fathom the thought of losing everything he had worked so hard to acquire over fifteen years. She had to go and he was fueled with the adrenaline to get rid of her ass post haste. In the back of the house, Pandora ran through the huge yard and into a baseball field compiled of high snow mounds and dried up dirt.

"Pandora!" Ivan yelled putting his feet to the snow running as if he were in a track meet, "I just wanna talk."

Her ears heard him but her mind was
listening as she trucked through the calf length
snow shivering and wishing she had enough time
to grab a coat. She checked her pockets making
sure she still had the four hundred dollars that Oxy
had given her earlier. When she felt the tops of the
paper, she pressed harder to make it to the
streetlights ahead of her where all of the late night
traffic was. Her gut told her that even though they
were dead set on killing her they were not bold
enough to shoot her in front of a ton of witnesses.
She ran as fast and as hard as she could in the thick
hard snow only minutes away from salvation.

BANG!

Ivan had taken another shot at her and
missed again purposely, hoping it would slow her
down. Not only was he sending out warning
signals to Pandora to stop but also he wanted to
make sure that if Oxy was nearby she heard it
letting her know that he was on the job. He was not
overweight but he drank so much alcohol that his
body was not conditioned and unable to withstand
long periods of exercise. Even though he found
himself slowing down he pushed his body like
none other, desperate not to let her get away.

"Oh Shit!" Pandora breathed as she found
herself closer to her destination.

"Pandora!"

There were absolutely no cars on the street and the nearest store was almost two miles away. She knew she would never make it with them hot on her trail and needed to find a way out fast. Her arms moved forward and backward faster to help her legs move faster. It worked and in the distance she could see a pack of cars coming up. She was not that far from the street and began waving her arms wildly hoping to catch the attention of someone that would stop and help her out.

"Oh God! Please! Help! Stop, please!" Pandora yelled as she neared the street, "Stop, please!"

"Hey, are you alright young lady?" An older man with salt colored hair slowed rolling his window down.

"Please wait!" Pandora was a few feet away from the car, pushing hard to make it those last few steps.

"What you running from, princess?" The elderly man asked. "I gots me a shot gun in my trunk. You need some help girl?"

"No, please can you just drive off please!" Pandora requested very much out of breath.

The old man looked in the field and could see no one in the distance. He was beginning to believe that she was on some kind of drug and was losing her mind. She stared off into the dark field of snow and had to admit she could not see where Ivan went just that quickly. He was hot on her toes but just like that he was gone. As the old man drove off slower than a turtle who needed to take a shit she couldn't help but think of how lucky she was to get away, exhaling a sigh of relief. Pandora kept looking back behind them trying to see if they were being followed but it was just too hard to tell especially at night.

"Where are you going, princess?"

"Just keep driving. I'll tell you where to turn," Pandora stressed.

Chapter 15: "You are so fucked right now." — Diamond

"Did you see that bitch try to rip my fucking hair out, Tommy?" Diamond laughed as she sat in the driver's seat of the car.

"Yeah, lucky I came along or else you would have gotten your ass beat," Tommy chuckled slapping Diamond on her leg.

It was the first time that a man had touched her in any kind of sexual manner since before she was kicked out on the street and left for dead at a bus stop. She gazed out the window into the back of the car parked in front of her thinking about the fact that Tommy was a great guy; she just met him at the wrong point in time in her life. He was tall standing almost at six feet with a slender build. He was black but extra light skinned with smooth wavy baby hair and a smile that could last a lifetime. He rocked a fresh pair of the new wheat suede Timberlands but he wore a huge blue jumpsuit under his think bubble coat.

"So what's with the getup? What do you do exactly?" Diamond asked sparking conversation.

"I work at Midway airport. I fuel the planes."

"Oh that's gotta be cool."

"Yeah," Tommy replied.

"Well, thanks for following me home. I truly appreciate you helping me back there and sitting here talking with me to calm me down. You're a really cool dude," Diamond complimented turning towards him.

"And you're a very beautiful woman. You know, despite all the scratches and bald spots from the fight," Tommy smirked fake punching her lower chin.

"Don't play with me. I don't have any scratches or bald spots. You got me twisted boo. I'm a beauty," Diamond testified.

"That you are," Tommy agreed as he leaned in giving her a peck on her cheek.

"Um, well I guess I will be going in the house now. Thanks again for everything and I will definitely be giving you a call. Maybe we can go on a date sometime," Diamond recited nervously.

Her palms were sweaty and her knees were shaking. It was the first time she had ever been in the presence of a man and don't feel like her average over sexy self. She did not want to flirt with him or throw her tits in his face. Her pussy did not even make its normal throb from being near him. It was then that she knew she did have a conscious buried underneath her hard exterior.

"Wait a minute. So you not gonna pay me for saving you from getting your ass whooped?"

"Pay you? You want money for saving me from a fight? Wow," Diamond laughed reaching into her pocket.

"Naw," Tommy said smiling and halting her hand from its tight pocket dig, "Not that kind of payment. I don't want your money."

"Oh...Tommy there's something you need to..."

"Shh. It's okay. I get it. I'll be gentle," Tommy smiled as he moved in for the kill.

"No, that's not it," Diamond said pushing him back, rather annoyed by his persistence, "And we just met. You think I'm just gonna sleep with you?"

"Well ain't that what you were getting your ass whooped for? Because you were a hoe sleeping with someone's husband," Tommy reached over to the side of her seat letting her backrest all the way back.

"Stop, Tommy. Now I'm trying to be nice,"

Diamond fought pushing him off of her realizing that he was slowly making his way on top of her.

Tommy stepped one foot over to her foot space and allowed the next foot to follow as he wiggled his manhood out from the button up space on the jumpsuit with one hand and holding Diamond's mouth closed with the other. For his build he was rather strong unbuttoning her pants and yanked them down forcefully. She never thought he would get them down but once he did she tried to lock her yellow legs together. He reached down prying them open and maneuvering in between.

"You don't want to do this," Diamond suggested feeling as though her attempts to stop him would be futile.

"Shut the fuck up! You hoes are all the same. You wanna lead a nigga on and then when he gets good and ready you wanna turn a nigga off," Tommy panted, rubbing Diamond's tits roughly.

"I didn't lead you on. I just fucking thanked you for your help. I did nothing to deserve this shit," Diamond's voice was surprisingly calm.

"Really, well I promise you'll enjoy it."

Diamond closed her eyes hoping to die right

then and there. She did not want tears to fall from her eyes and show that jerk that he had broken her. He was not worth her tears or pain. She could feel his manhood rub against the outside of her opening threatening to break it open and as he eased it in Diamond became overly depressed. Tommy rammed inside of her slow yet deep being sure to tap her uterus with every thrust.

"Scream for me baby," Tommy moaned. "But not too loud."

"You're making a huge mistake. You are so fucked right now," Diamond stated keeping her eyes closed.

Tommy was very uncomfortable in the position that he was in so he picked Diamond's legs up and shifted them around to the passenger side seat along with his legs remaining inside of her. Her head hit her seat feeling him reposition himself inside of her. She just lied there like a bag of potatoes, dead and lifeless. He could have killed her right then and she would not have cared one bit. But there was one detail that Diamond had up on him and it would definitely be a lifelong lesson learned for him.

"You are a stupid motherfucka," Diamond whispered lightly.

"What? What the fuck did you just say?"

"You are stupid!" Diamond yelled like he was hard of hearing.

"But I got this pussy though. So now who's stupid?" Tommy laughed licking his index and middle fingertips then sent them to rub Diamond's clit to make her hot.

"It's still you. Cause I got AIDS, MOTHERFUCKA!" Diamond taunted at the top of her lungs.

"You're lying. I wasn't born yesterday. You ain't gotta lie baby, I'll be done in a minute."

"I'm not lying," Diamond whispered as she turned her head to the side no longer smiling.

He looked down at her facial expression still pumping inside of her and waiting for her demeanor to change. When it never did he became concerned that there might have been some truth to what she was saying. It never dawned on him that she could be a diseased whore. He was just worried about getting his rocks off.

"What?" Tommy said backing off slowly, trembling at the thought. "Don't play with me bitch."

"I'm not fucking playing you damn asshole!"

"Bitch you got AIDS?" Tommy asked hyperventilating as he leaned back ripping his piece out of her without hesitation.

"Maybe you should learn to respect women and then you won't have problems like this…ASSHOLE!"

Boom! Boom! Boom! Boom!

Tommy began pounding on her face horribly. One after the other he pounded his fists into her face hoping to kill her right where she lay. With every punch, he found himself growing angrier hoping to disfigure her face beyond recognition. Diamond felt no pain even though it hurt like hell. She refused to fight the urge to die and looked at this as a blessing to get away from the torture that is life. Tears formed in her eyes and the only sounds she made was a little wincing here and there to let him know she was not quite dead yet.

The car door opened abruptly and a set of hands pulled Tommy out by his legs tossing his ass up in the cold night air and banging his mouth on the bottom part of the doorway. Mountains of blood flew from his mouth along with three of his front teeth. He held his hand up trying to catch the mess spewing from his mouth but nearly choking on it he had to release it onto the dirty white snow.

"Get your nasty ass out of here motherfucka!" Pandora yelled kicking him in his ass before allowing him to get up and race to his car.

"Y'all some crazy ass bitches! Fuck y'all man! Y'all gone die! You hear me? You bitches are dead!"

"Tell me something I don't know," Diamond said opening the glove compartment, taking out the gun she had stashed in there from before.

The sound of Pandora's voice alerted her to one thing, it was about to go down. She checked her face in the rearview mirror as she pulled her pants up and straightened the rest of her clothes. Her right eye was swollen but it was not closed shut, she considered that a good thing as she tried to keep an eye on her sister while she slid the gun down in her pants feeling the cold metal on her twat. The skin on her face was busted but it was bleeding badly, in her mind she was fine and ready to settle the score.

"Come on and get out here, Diamond. You know what I want and I ain't got all day," Pandora commanded as she checked the streets for suspicious activity.

"So, I see you made it out of jail. They

finally let you out because you dropped the soap too many damn times. They said you liked that shit too much bitch," Diamond laughed as she exited the car, walking straight up to her.

"Damn bitch. He was about to make a meat sandwich out of your face. You look like straight shit."

"Thank you. I appreciate that."

"Fuck the bullshit, though. Where's my fucking money?"

"I have no idea what the fuck you are talking about, sis," Diamond responded casually.

"Diamond, look at you. No one's going to want you, and that money you got ain't even gonna be enough to fix your face. So what do you say? Just give it to me, I promise that you and Lex won't get hurt," Pandora lied.

"Ah yes, your fuck buddy, sorry she couldn't be here today but she's a little indisposed at the moment," Diamond laughed.

Pandora's patience began to diminish. She was not there to play footsy with her sister; she was there to get her money so she could get the hell out of Dodge. She looked Diamond up and down noticing that she was living a rough life.

Why guys always wanted to rape her, she had no idea, but just because they were feuding did not mean she would allow some pompous jerk to get away with that shit.

"I saved you sis. You owe me. If it weren't for me you'd be dead by now. I don't know why I'm always playing Captain Save-A-Hoe to you ungrateful broads but I do and so now you owe me." Pandora paused to let it sink in. "And all you have to give me is what's rightfully mine."

Diamond felt something hard and crunchy in her mouth. She used her tongue to fiddle around with it and noticed that one of her teeth had fallen out from the powerful blows her face endured. She spit the tooth out on the ground along with a glob of bloody saliva. She looked up into Pandora's face and spit the blood towards her but it missed her by a millimeter. It disappointed her and pissed Pandora off to the max.

"Not only was that nasty but that was disrespectful. Now I'm only gonna ask you one more time, nicely, or else I'm gonna be the bitch stomping mud holes in your ass with your face on the concrete this time," Pandora growled horridly. "Now where the fuck is my got damn money?"

Chapter 16: *"Pray for me for what, Diamond?" — Pandora*

Diamond spit out more blood then moved her mouth like she was an old man chewing tobacco. Pandora was so smug that she thought she could intimidate anyone but Diamond had been through too much shit to fall for her threats. The two women stood in the briskly blowing wind with tiny ice particles assaulting their skin, focusing on each other's every move. The artic breeze began to prick through their skin and attack their blood stream but neither of them would admit that they could feel it. Their stare off appeared icy enough.

"You sure are a relentless bitch, ain't ya Pandora? It's a shame; I used to be happy to call you my twin once," Diamond said shaking her head.

"I'm not here to get sentimental with you. I just want my got damn money and you can go on living your mundane existence broke as hell."

"And yet, you'll never be the same again."

"Don't make me ask you again, dear Diamond."

"Fine, I'm done fighting with you. I'm done trying to get you to see how much you've changed and I'm done trying to save your ass from yourself. So if that money is all you want, you can have it," Diamond uttered, "But the shit will never bring you happiness."

"Yeah, we'll just see about that," Pandora's lips dripped with greed as she looked around unable to wait to get her hands on it, "Okay, so where is it?"

"Oh, I buried it so no one could find it. You didn't think I was dumb enough to keep it on me, did you?" Diamond shrugged as she limped around to the driver's side of the car, "Come on hop in. I'll take you right to it, but you're gonna have to dig it up. You know, me being injured and all."

"Where the fuck is it, Diamond? I don't have time for games."

"I buried it in the back of the Dan Ryan Woods on Western. Come on, it won't take long," Diamond informed her while dipping down into the driver's seat, revving the car up.

Pandora looked into the car, standing at the passenger side door wondering what Diamond's angle was. She did not know if she was being truthful about where she had stashed the money.

All she knew was if Diamond had faked her out, she would definitely pay for it much worse than what she just experienced. She slid into the seat closing the door looking over into her face for any sign of bullshit. It was hard to read any expression from her face since her lips were slowly swelling up and the right side of her face appeared badly disfigured.

"It better be out there Diamond. I'm telling you…" Pandora shook her head and bit her bottom lip.

"Don't get your panties all in a bunch, it's out there. You just have to dig it up, shouldn't be too deep though. You're a strong girl," Diamond smiled as she drove on down the road.

The car was virtually silent for the remainder of the ride back to the city with Pandora keeping her hands folded as if she was giving every move Diamond made her undivided attention. If she were caught slipping, it would not be for lack of that. Diamond swerved rather roughly off of the 87th Street expressway anxious to get to the woods and get this over with. She kept a close eye on the passenger seat making sure her dear sister did not make any sudden moves but she slowly eased off knowing that Pandora would not do anything as long as her money hung in the balance. Pandora, on the other hand, could not think of nothing else but throwing Diamond in the whole that the money came out of, burying her alive.

"The Woods is on Western, right?" Pandora asked becoming impatient.

"Girl, don't act like you don't know where it's at. You grew up here, shit," Diamond retorted annoyed that she had the audacity to rush her driving.

There was not a cloud in the sky or traffic on the ground for a Thursday evening. It was strange but convenient seeing as though somebody was about to die and Diamond surely did not need any witnesses to her crime. She looked deep within herself trying to find the least bit of remorse for her sister. She wanted to see if she could feel anything for her that she could use to force her to change before it boiled down to her last breath.

"Now you can turn up in that lot right there and drive all the way around. I swear my fucking money better be in here D."

"You so damn blinded by that damn money that you can't see the life that you're missing out on."

"What? Girl shut the fuck up with all of that shit. Nobody wanna talk about that shit, but you,"

Pandora spat emphasizing her speech with her left hand, "If you was a real bitch you wouldn't have fucking gone against the grain."

And just like that, Diamond halted the car. She threw it in park hard enough to make Pandora jerk forward nearly hitting her head on the ceiling of the car then shut the ignition off staring out of the windshield at darkness. Her limbs were unable to move and she felt a great gloom come over her. The blood in her veins raced and her heart slowed its rate as if it were ready to die. Pandora looked over at her wondering what the hell she was doing as she waved her hand in front of her face to snap her out of her daze.

"What the fuck are you doing?" Pandora asked unpleasantly.

"We're here," Diamond replied calmly never breaking her eyes from the darkness or flinching an inch. "It's straight back there. It's in between two trees that are close together."

"Well get the hell out and let's go, shit. I ain't got all day," Pandora howled eagerly. "Where's the shovel?"

"Oh, uh, I don't have one. But you can dig it out with your hands."

"My hands?"

"Damn, it's not that deep I told you. Let's go," Diamond said waiting for her to walk off ahead of her.

The two women trucked through the thin layer of snow using only their good judgment and the moonlight to guide them along the way. A few feet out Pandora began to wonder if Diamond even remembered where the place was since it felt like they were just walking aimlessly. In the distance, Pandora squint her eyes attempting to focus them on the large figure ahead. She believed that she had found the tree pattern that Diamond described, secretly becoming overjoyed that she would soon be reunited with the green she had hustled so hard to get. Her legs seemed to take on a mind of their own, as she found herself running up ahead. But her excitement was short lived when she reached the area and realized that the tree pattern she had seen was actually a mirage, an illusion of the night. Heated by the trick her mind and eyes had played on her she turned to face her casually striding sister.

"That's not it! That's not it!" Pandora looked around hysterically. "Where is it?"

"You know when we were little; we used to do everything together. Do you remember that?" Diamond paused for an answer but when she received nothing but heavy breathing she continued on, "I used to braid your hair and I even taught you how to ride a bike. You were so naïve then and I guess you still are."

"What?"

"Pandora, you are so self-absorbed that you can't see the difference between the truth and a lie," Diamond smirked as she revealed the gun from out of the front of her pants.

"What's that, a gun? You've got to be kidding me right? What are you gonna do Diamond? HUH? You gonna be a coward and shoot me? Anybody can shoot someone but can you kill someone with your bare fucking hands? That's what separates the girls from the women," Pandora stalled.

"You know if this was a few months ago, all of your bullshit talk might have had some sort of influence on me, but looking at you now...all I wanna do is pray for you," Diamond said raising the gun up to her sister's head.

Pandora moved in closer giving Diamond a good shot without any illusions making it difficult for her to miss. She grabbed her hair swinging it back behind her and held her chin up waiting for her to pull the trigger.

"Pray for me for what, Diamond?"

"For your soul not to go straight to hell, you should stop by heaven to see everything you will be missing."

"You don't have the fucking balls to shoot me, bitch. You're weak. You're wretched. You've always been! That's why I had to carry us because you were too weak to fucking do it your damn self and you are the oldest!" Pandora bellowed, "You're so fucking bad then do it!"

"Shut up, Pandora!"

"What are you waiting for, just do it!"

Pandora rushed Diamond knocking her to her back, then jumps on top of her. The gun flew out of Diamond's hand landing a few feet behind then. Pandora is sitting on top of Diamond's torso pressing all of her weight on her to keep her down as she scratched and clawed at her face.

Diamond reached up grabbing her hands to keep her from attacking, but she was very fast and Diamond's equilibrium was still off from the beating she had endured no less than an hour before. The bubble jacket Diamond adorned prevented her from being distracted from the feel of the wet, slushy snow and mud, but as Pandora yanked on it she began to wish she had left it in the car.

Pandora stood up planting her feet on each side of her head never releasing the coat for a second. She twisted it to no end making sure it was nice and tight before pulling it close to her neck strangling her to no end.

Diamond struggled and fought punching her arms, hoping to break her strength or at least distract her so that she would let up a little and focus on stopping her hands. Pandora was no fool. She continued to squeeze much like an Anaconda would its prey, yanking and pressing harder waiting for her to give up and pass out. It had begun to sink in that she was never going to get the money from Diamond, which meant she had to focus on the weaker sister, Lexi. Diamond held her breath for as long as she could while trying to fight the affects that made her head dizzy. She focused all of her energy on swinging her fists aiming for her face but was unable to reach it. Just as she was about to go down for the count a loud ringing engulfed her ears.

"Give up bitch! Give up!" Pandora gritted through her teeth as she squeezed with all of her might.

Pandora grinned viciously, allowing drool to fall from her mouth for the taste of Diamond's blood. When she envisioned herself killing Diamond, she did not imagine that it would be that satisfying. It was a hunger that she longed for as she anticipated the moment her frail body went limp and she took her very last breath. But Diamond was a fighter and was determined to live. She was not going to go down without giving Pandora a run for her money. Her breathing slowed and she could see death in the distance but she was not ready to go. *'Hold up, not just yet,'* she thought to herself as she reached up pulling down on Pandora's arms to bring a little relief to her sore neck.

"Just die bitch! Let go!" Pandora taunted.

Her hands loosened their grip and dropped Diamond to the ground awkwardly. She turned around to see if she could see someone but there was no one there. Diamond coughed grasping her neck in relief trying to regain her strength and functioning as she peered out at the gun lying no less than a few feet from her. As she crawled towards it she witnessed Pandora fall to her knees screaming in pure agony. There was no time to focus on what happened to her as Diamond neared the gun grabbing it, cradling it like a helpless child.

"Not so bad now are you baby?" Oxy laughed walking up to assess the scene.

"Oxy! Why the fuck are you doing this to me?" Pandora shrieked in sheer pain as she clenched her right leg trying to stop the blood from spewing out.

"Don't ask questions you already know the answer to Pandora. You were supposed to be mine. You were supposed to remain pure and then you go and fuck Ivan," Oxy hollered pointing to Ivan.

Ivan stood there pointing the gun towards Pandora. The darkness made it hard for him to gaze at her beauty, leaving no room for him to be distracted or feel remorseful. Tears flowed from Pandora's eyes as thoughts scrolled through her head of not being ready to die yet. She felt there were so many other things she needed to do before she went. And then it hit her. That was the very thing Diamond was trying to implant in her head. She sighed coming to the notion that the old saying was definitely true. A hard head did make a soft ass.

"It wasn't personal, baby. It was all business," Pandora panted, smiling nervously.

"Just shut up! I loved you, talking all that shit about marriage. Did you think I was stupid?" Oxy scratched her head profusely nearly drawing blood. "You...Ivan...Did you think I was going to let you get away with that? HUH?"

"I...I..."

"You what?"

"I thought I imagined you standing there. I didn't know you really did see us," Pandora cried and begged, "Oxy please, I'm sorry baby."

Pandora looked over at Diamond clenching the gun in her hands wondering who the fuck these people were and if they were going to kill her too just because she was a witness. Oxy paced the snow, kicking it in her ex-lover's direction hoping to make her feel like the dirt she was.

"Even if I wanted to, I couldn't save you. It's a shame too. Your pussy was very sweet," Oxy confessed as she turned to sway away, disgusted by her face and spoke coolly, "Shoot her!"

Bang! Bang!

Ivan slugged two in her chest aiming for her heart. Oxy turned around watching as Pandora laid spread out on the ground finding it difficult to breathe. Diamond rose slowly from the ground, clenching the piece tightly, looking down in Pandora's face. Pandora refused to look her in the face wanting the last thing she saw in this world to be the iridescent beauty of the pale moonlight. Her chest slowed and her fingers ceased to wiggle but Diamond could still hear her faint short breaths seeping from her young lips.

"Breathe dog, breathe," Diamond encouraged.

Pandora took her final breath turning her eyes to Diamond at the last moment only able to catch a silhouette. Her body was affixed like something out of a horror movie as Diamond kissed her goodbye on her head.

"Good riddance to bad rubbish," she muttered as she looked up into the shadows of Oxy and Ivan and slowly raised her gun releasing the safety, "Ay, I don't want any motherfucking trouble."

"Don't you now," Oxy replied crossing her arms.

"I never saw either of you and you didn't see me. It's dark out here anyway," Diamond insisted knowing that even if she did not get both of them she would be happy with at least one.

Oxy smacked her lips, shaking her head at Diamond as she lightly caressed the side of Ivan's arm, "Come on daddy. Let's go."

Diamond exhaled heavily like she had just been reborn. She lowered the gun keeping her finger on the trigger just until they were out of her sight. The entire time she had not felt the cold crusty air of the woods but at that moment an apocalyptic breeze seemed to be surrounding her. She slid the gun back into her pants securing the safety again. Her eyes took one last look at the person she once shared a mother, a face and thick blood with then gradually turned and headed back towards the car.

Chapter 17: "You got it right. Don't be any man's fool." — Diamond

Diamond sat in the car looking around at the emptiness of the parking lot before revving up and pulling off. She did not want to be noticed by any cops on their late night beat, coming out of an already closed for the day forest preserve. She peeled slowly out of the lot headed North on Western Avenue, being sure to check her mirrors for any followers or the police. Her movements were erratic and her nerves were beyond a mess. She needed to calm down spotting a Citgo gas station on the corner coming ahead and pulled into it shutting off the ignition to breathe.

She exited the car and entered the mini mart sluggishly hoping to find something with some alcohol in it. It was the only thing she could think of to calm her nerves down. At the counter, the Pakistani young man looked as if he did not trust her. The odd way she walked through the store as she found her two Red Bulls and returned to the front seemed off.

"Yeah, take this and keep the change," Diamond growled as she tossed him a twenty dollar bill then snatched her drinks off the counter and headed back outside.

Her weary legs slid back into the driver's seat as she cracked one of the drinks open throwing it back like it was water. The wait for the rush was killing her as she tossed the can in the garbage can just outside the car. She was about to open the other can we the phone rang.

"Hello?"

"Hey D, where you been? I've been calling you like crazy," Lexi asked worriedly, relieved to hear her voice.

"Naw, yeah girl I'm good. I have just been through one hell of a night," Diamond laughed trying not to scare her.

"Well I waited for you to come back to the hospital. I thought you were going to pick me up but you stood me up...again."

"I'm so sorry lil' sis, I don't have an excuse for not being there for you either and you know what, starting today I'm going to strive to be a better big sister to you, okay?"

"Yes, Diamond, but you are already a great big sister. You're tough but you keep me on my toes."

"As do you, Hun," Diamond smiled brightly no matter how badly it hurt.

"So, have you heard from Pandora yet?"

"Lex, don't freak out when I say this. You gotta promise me you won't cry or freak out, promise?" Diamond closed her eyes.

"Diamond, you're scaring me. What's going on and where are you? Are you okay?" Lexi rambled.

"See, I just asked you not to freak out."

"Okay, I'm calm, tell me," Lexi closed her eyes, took a deep breath and braced herself.

"I got a feeling that we won't be hearing much from Pandora anytime soon."

The phone went silent. Diamond waited to give her time to process the harsh information she just received. Lexi being a very emotional person felt for people even if she did not know them. She wanted to give her all the time she needed in order for her to begin the healing process and move on with her life but feared it may take more time than the phone call could provide. On the other end of the line, Lexi clenched her hand over her mouth so she did not blurt out any sudden gasps or cries. At the end of the day, she knew Pandora was like a flesh eating virus, once it spread all over you it claims your life.

"That's a shame," she replied remaining calm.

"Huh? You're not going burst into tears or throw up or nothing?" Diamond asked beyond shocked by her response.

"I'm growing up, diva," Lexi laughed, "I know she was a bad seed. Nothing or no one was going to change that. Once good girls go bad they're gone forever."

"Straight up," Diamond agreed, "Well I'm so proud of you lil' sis. Girl you're gonna make me cry over here."

"Well save your tears because I've got news too. Are you sitting down?" Lexi smiled.

"Yes but Alexis, if you tell me that Kojack proposed and you said yes, I'm gonna run this car off the side of the road and end it all. I fucking swear!" Diamond was joking but she hoped Lexi knew she meant it.

"Huh? Damn D, why you always gotta fuck some shit up? Can I finish my news please?"

"Okay, I'm sorry. You're right. Whatever it is I support you and I'm happy for you. So...what is it?" Diamond bit her lip hoping she would not regret asking that question.

"I'm pregnant!" Lexi exclaimed looking around to see if Kojack was still in the bathroom.

"Oh my God! That's great baby! I'm so happy for you," Diamond lied, "So what does Kojack think about this?"

"He wants to be in the baby's life and blah, blah, blah."

"So what are you going to do for real, Lex?"

"I haven't really decided yet. But I told him that I was getting an abortion. He hurt me bad D. and I don't know if I can get over that. Fool me once, shame on you. But fool me twice and we're done," Lexi lowered her head trying not to cry.

"Sometimes niggas are gonna hurt you bad boo. But it's up to you as a woman to know what you will stand for and what you won't. They will only do to us what we allow them to do," Diamond educated her sister, putting on her 'big sister' cap.

"I know, I know."

"You got it right, don't be any man's fool," Diamond lectured rubbing the stress off of her scalp.

The phone went silent as the knowledge sunk into Lexi's brain. She needed that sisterly advice, a sort of kick in the ass so she did not keep making the same mistakes over and over again. Her hand grazed her belly hoping she would also make the right decision when it came down to the life inside of her. Her confusion bordered on the line of being a hypocrite by telling Diamond not to abort her baby when she was now thinking of doing that very thing.

"So anyway, have you given any thought to keeping your baby?"

"Oh, I don't know, Lex. I'm not equipped to take care of a baby and I got this disease. I...I just don't know."

"But I will be there to help you. Hell, I don't know what I'm doing either but we can help each other. That's what sisters are for, right?" Lexi laughed as did Diamond, "People live long, happy lives with Aids, D."

"I know but it's not that. It's the thought of knowing that one day, any day; I could die and leave that little kid on this earth without a mother or a father all alone. We know that feeling all too well and that's something I couldn't live with each day I am alive," Diamond felt a large quantity of tears build up in the ducts of her eyes.

"But the baby won't be alone Diamond because it will have me. I would never let you die no matter if you're here in the flesh or in spirit.

Don't you know that?"

"Yeah, yeah, I know. I just can't wrap my mind around the thought is all? You know momma left us and all we had was the Pastor and I know you wouldn't do anything to hurt the baby. I just need more time, Lex."

Lexi could not understand why the decision was so hard for Diamond. She was not in the predicament that she had gotten herself into and would actually have preferred if she had no idea who her child's father was. It would have made her decision a lot easier, keeping the baby and not having to worry about sharing it with someone who was only going to continue to break her heart. Her love for Kojack was real but it seemed his love was only convenient when it affected him.

"I understand," Lexi lied, "But please while you're thinking about it, can you at least go to the doctor in the morning and get the meds? You or the baby won't survive without it regardless of your decision."

"Ugh, if it will make you happy, little sis!" Diamond accentuated playfully rolling her eyes.

The two girls laughed like they used to back in the day when times were stressful but simpler. They fell into a conversation about their childhoods, reminiscing about how much fun they used to have sneaking out the windows and playing pranks on unsuspecting pedestrians from the roof. It warmed both of their hearts to be able to talk to each other and love each other as sisters were supposed to without all of the bickering, fighting, and backstabbing. It felt real and even though neither of them wanted to get all mushy over the phone they were both thinking the same thing at the same time, I love you.

"Alright sis, I'm going to get out of this damn gas station. The fucking foreign dude is looking at me funny through his bulletproof window," Diamond joked and cackled. "Where are you right now?"

"I'm at Kojack's office with him. He took me out to dinner at Longhorn Steakhouse and so we just made it to his office. He says he needs to talk to me about something but he needed to stop off and pick some papers up first," Lexi replied curling her lips and turning up her nose as she watched him step out of the bathroom spraying air freshener, "Well he's done stinking up the bathroom, girl. I guess I gotta go too."

Diamond frowned as she listened to Kojack's movements in the background. She hated the way he was stringing her sister along with his wishy washy ways but did not know how to tell her to axe him without getting into a full-fledged argument like before. It was going to take for him to hurt her so bad that she never wanted to see his face again for Lexi to wake up and smell the coffee that love was never going to be enough for a man like Kojack. He would never truly love her the way she wanted to be loved because of their differences. How could she tell her sister to stay away when she was clearly blinded by the exact same thing that caught him in the first place, wild and crazy, spontaneous sex?

"Okay girl," Diamond grimaced, "Are y'all going to his crib afterwards?"

"Yeah we'll definitely be there," Lexi confirmed.

"Okay cool. Well I'll meet you guys there. I'm gonna run to this Mickey D's up the street and hit the drive through hard and then I'll be there."

"That's Wassup, alright then."

"Hey Lex."

"Love you too, sis," she smiled as Diamond sent her love right back before disconnecting the call.

Diamond started the car, looking back at the gas station attendant throwing him the most horrid stink face she could make as she pulled off. She broke a left heading back North on Western Avenue feeling her stomach growl as the bright yellow McDonald's arches slowly came into view. It was none other than the baby inside forcing her to acknowledge its presence. With hunger pangs roaring an earthquake through to her back, she began to think rationally about the points Lexi made. It was easy for her to deny she was right and fight her logic since being difficult was in her nature. But the truth was she was overly devastated that she had gotten pregnant and with the lifestyle she led, a baby was a bad addition. She knew Lexi would never be able to tame a beast like that even if she tried.

The stop light on 79th and Western seemed to be taking forever, as she hawked at the teens crossing the street laughing loudly, shouting obscenities. Diamond frowned at their antics feeling for sure that her kid would come out even worse than they were. Her eyes rolled to the back of her head, her lips smacked together in disgust at the very thought of raising a disrespectful spoiled brat. As the light turned green, she took off almost like she was in the Kentucky Derby ready to get her grub on. Not even halfway down the block, she looked over at the rinky dink diner across the street, Nicky's Restaurant.

"What the hell?"

Chapter 18: "I'm coming momma." — Diamond

Diamond busted a full on U-turn driving her car right into the bus terminal right next to the small rectangular shaped restaurant, without care of who did not like that she did so. She jumped out of the car walking dead up to the short stocky lady locking the diner door and her uniformed husband standing beside her. Her lips were immobile as were her hands. Her nerves were as cool as could be but her heart rate beat faster and faster by the second. She could not fix her lips to say anything and once they turned around to face her they could not believe their eyes.

"Sergeant Sutter's, just the man I wanted to see; the fucking man of the hour," Diamond rambled laughing in a crazy manner.

"Diamond, what are you doing here?" Sutter's whispered as he leaned in whispering, "You see my wife Kathy standing here."

"What the fuck are you whispering to her for?" Kathy scolded gut punching him with her elbow.

"Yeah what the fuck are you whispering for, Sutter's? She didn't tell you that we've talked already?" Diamond asked nearly out of breath with excitement.

"Look bitch. You've got some nerve coming up here to my place of business with this bullshit. Now you're lucky that I don't have any customers in there and I've just locked up. But if you come around here again, I will have you arrested," Kathy said as Sutter's walked a few feet to his unmarked squad car parked on the side of the building.

"Have me arrested? Bitch I will press charges against you for assault."

"What are you talking about? I'm not the one who disfigured your face," Kathy laughed as she attempted to walk off but found herself halted by a rough shove.

"So what bitch? You thought that shit was over? Like you was just gonna pull my fucking hair out and get away with that shit?" Diamond yelled feeling herself becoming more heated than ever.

Her intention was not to go over to them and start a fight but to curse the day Sutter's was born for giving her a disease she would never be able to get rid of. She was so young and had her whole life ahead of her but the more she thought about her illness the more depressed she became believing her life was over. The fun, the dating, the love, and the sex she could be having was all stripped away because of him. She blamed the entire reason why her life was so fucked up on him regardless of if he was solely to blame or not.

"Really? You're doing all of this because you want payback for getting your ass whooped earlier?" Kathy laughed, "Honey you are truly a little girl. I don't have time for this so if you came down here to waste your time then go ahead because I'm not fighting. I just got off of work, I'm tired, my feet hurt and I don't have time for this shit."

"So because you don't feel like fighting, I'm supposed to accept that? Did you care about my feelings earlier? I wasn't trying to fight you and all you kept doing was fucking with me," Diamond protested as she raised her fists up blocking her face.

"You know what, if hitting me is going to make you feel better then go ahead but I'm not fighting. So if you're going to swing then swing but know that I'm having you arrested," Kathy folded her chunky arms.

"Ugh!" Diamond's rage got the best of her as she launched her arm punching Kathy dead in her nose. "Now what bitch? Let's go!"

"Hey! Alright Diamond, this has gone on long enough. Now go home!" Sutter's said walking up to his wife, checking to see if she was okay.

"Get the fuck off of me. I'm fine," Kathy shoved him as she searched her purse for a tissue to clean the blood dripping from her nose, "I'm about to go in here and fix myself and when I get back she needs to be in handcuffs on her way to the station."

"Okay," Sutter's responded.

"I mean it!" Kathy sneered as she turned the key to the door of the restaurant and entered locking it behind her.

"I said okay got damn it. Now gone in there and fix yourself up there," Sutter's ordered becoming frustrated as he turned back towards Diamond, "Why the fuck are you here?"

"That bitch assaults me at a fucking gas station, in the suburbs mind you, and I'm supposed to just let that shit go? Awe hell naw, you got me fucked up Sutter's," Diamond spat shoving him forcefully to piss him off. "But off her and on you, so you got AIDS son of a bitch? You got motherfucking AIDS and you spreading the shit around the city of Chicago?"

"Keep your got damn voice down dammit! I

am a respectable man of the law. And you...you just some hoe that gave it up when I wanted it," Sutter's argued grabbing her by the arm luring her over to his car.

"I was good at being your hoe as long as you paid for it you bitch ass motherfucking crooked ass cop! Ay, y'all this motherfucka is a crooked ass cop who been selling the lockup drugs to the drug dealers!" Diamond yelled to the streets as she fought to keep his hands off of her mouth.

The entire scene did not look good for Sergeant Sutter's as he was dressed completely in uniform and was being seen manhandling a female in the streets. He was pulling her left and right as she used her weight to maneuver around his grasps. Diamond reached up slapping him in his head knocking his hat off of his head setting his anger off tenfold.

"Look now bitch! Take your dumb ass home before I lock you up!"

"What you locking me up for? Because you gave me AIDS or because you fuck with niggas?" Diamond stopped fighting to watch the priceless reaction on his face, stunned, "Yeah your wife spilled the beans on everything boo boo. You done fucked up, royally!"

"She doesn't know what she's talking about.

That's a got damn lie," Sutter's retorted bending over to pick up his hat.

"She showed me the pictures, Sutter's. You're cold busted and you need your ass whooped. You ruined my fucking life and I hate you!"

"Naw, I ain't do nothing like that now, gal get on. We're done here."

"No we ain't done. We ain't done till I say we done motherfucka you're gonna listen to me," Diamond said hauling off again, planting slaps to his face repeatedly as he backed away.

Kathy came back out witnessing the brawl between the two and quickly felt overwhelmed with grief and embarrassment. She strolled over to the commotion tapping him on his shoulder giving him a look that would kill ten men. He knew what it meant but he did not want to address it while he was fighting off Diamond's blows to his face.

"I thought I said arrest her ass," Kathy said sucking her teeth.

"Why'd you tell her all of my business? That shit was for me and you that's it."

"I don't give a fuck about you being embarrassed. If you had kept it in your pants we wouldn't even be here!" Kathy stressed, watching Diamond as she kept finding little ways to fuck with him.

"I thought we talked about this Kat now," Sutter's yelled as access skin jiggled and turned red while raising his hand way up in the air bringing it down powerfully, striking Diamond right on her head, "Would you stop it?"

Diamond fell to the ground in the most excruciating pain imaginable. Her head pounded like a roaring thunderstorm was happening inside of it and her stomach was beginning to form tiny shots of cramps. She clenched her belly hunching over as the pain became more prevalent every time she moved. Her ears appeared to be falling deaf but her eyes caught a glimpse of Kathy's final words to Sutter's.

"That's it! I've had it!" Kathy reached up slapping him square in the face with all of her muscle, "I'm filing for divorce."

"Kathy! Kathy!" Sutter's called after her as she stormed off heading to her car parked directly in front of her business, "Kathy wait now, I need to say something."

Diamond's pain brewed hotter as she stood to face her assailant. He did not care about her pain or whether he had even hurt her at all. He was only focused on his wife whom he had carelessly spread his disease to.

"Agh!" Diamond sounded off limping over towards him, but paused in midstride.

She looked up noticing that her vision was now blurry and blood was gradually oozing from her nose. All at once, she became dizzy and nauseated. Diamond was worried that something was definitely wrong, not only with her but with the baby as well. She reached out her hand as she inched slowly over to Sutter's while he was pleading his case to Kathy. The tugging at his coat did not seem to interrupt him so she figured a slap upside his head would.

"Your little whore looks hurt," Kathy pointed out coolly, folding her arms paying no attention to what he was rambling on about.

"Sutter's, you fucking hit me too hard. I'm in pain..."

"Get the fuck off me! Go home Diamond and never come near me or my wife again!" Sutter's insisted as he pushed her down to the ground forcefully pointing in the direction of her car, "Leave us alone!"

"Sutter's, I'm pregnant you asshole!"

He did not seem to care, pretending not to have heard her. The blood from Diamond's nose dripped onto the dirty concrete as she stood on all fours having a hard time getting air into her passageways. Dry heaves circulated through her body like there was something more powerful to come but when it failed to do so Diamond rose slowly to her feet once more.

"You ruined my fucking life, Sutter's! You're a whore and disease carrying fungus!" Diamond yelled at the top of her lungs using all of her power so that people on every block could hear it.

"You know what. I warned you. I got something for hardheaded bitches like you. You just wait," Sutter's walked over to his car opening the door.

"Sutter's!" Diamond screeched.

Bang! Bang!

Even though she was in mounds of pain there was absolutely nothing wrong with her reflexes. She had whipped the gun out so fast that no one saw it coming. She dropped two into his potbelly stomach watching him drop to the floor clenching the wound and looking up at his wife.

"Hey you, drop the fucking weapon! Now!"

a cop yelled running from the terminal security stand, posting himself behind her car for a shield.

Diamond turned to him smiling like she had not one care in the world. It was funny to her that out of everyone out there that evening, no one had noticed Sutter's beat her down to a bloody pulp. She looked up into the night sky unable to see much closing her eyes to feel the frigid breeze beat against her skin. She looked back down focusing her attention back on what appeared to her as an off duty police officer. Diamond let out a sinister sounding laugh that would surely haunt the minds of every onlooker around for years to come.

"I said put the fucking gun down! This is your final warning!"

"I'm coming momma," Diamond whispered while raising the gun in the cop's direction.

Boom! Boom! Boom!

The officer's large gun ripped three shots off but only one mattered and that was the one that hit Diamond dead in her head nearly blowing off the top of her scalp. Sirens could be heard in the distance coming to aid the people involved in what some of the onlookers considered the craziest shit they ever seen. Kathy stood there as stiff as a board, simultaneously looking from her husband then back at Diamond's mangled carcass. Sutter's was slumped over motionless as the brave out of shape dark skinned cop came over to check his pulse.

"Is he dead?" Kathy asked silently clearing the phlegm out of her throat.

"I regret to inform you ma'am that I do not feel a pulse," the cop replied sincerely.

"Well that's what the fuck he gets. There goes your justice Diamond. Now rest in peace," she said while heading to her car determined to leave the scene and the past behind her.

Chapter 19: "AGHHHHHHHH!" — Lexi

Lexi sat on the sofa next to Kojack feeling her eyes grow heavy. They slowly drifted over to the door wondering why he had decided to settle in and watch a movie at his office rather than home. The movie was only about twenty minutes in and already she was bored from the old look and feel of the drama, Set It Off. She yawned propping her head up with her arm as she leaned on the armrest to keep from nodding off.

"Hey, you're falling asleep on the best part," Kojack nudged pointing to the TV with the remote in hand.

"Kojack, I'm tired. I just want to go home and get in the bed. I haven't been sleeping much these past few days. Besides, I keep hearing rattling in the back behind me. I think you got a rat in there or something," Lexi indicated as she stood getting a good long stretch in, "Why are we here? You said you needed papers and then we'd be out."

"My bad, I just thought we could spend a little time together and just kick it for a while."

Thud!

"You don't hear that shit?" Lexi side eyed.

"Naw, girl that baby got you going crazy. It's probably just the building settling or something. Besides there's nothing back there but a big ass closet," Kojack assured her as he waved off the sound, "Let's just focus on us."

"Focus on us? Okay, I don't know what's going on with you, but I can't sit here and pretend that there's nothing going on between us, like we don't have problems and junk," Lexi popped off.

"I know. I know. Lexi I've been procrastinating because I've got something to say to you and I don't know how to say it. I guess you can call me a bit of a chicken shit," he paused watching Lexi's facial expression read 'you got that right', "But I'm going to be a man right now and handle my business."

"Kojack, I've been hurt real bad and right now I'm tired and I think we just need to talk in the morning when both of our heads are clear."

"That'll only give you enough time to stick to your abortion decision and I really don't want that to happen," Kojack said grabbing her hand lovingly.

"What makes you think that I give a shit about what you want right now?" Lexi questioned as she turned around hearing the thud in the closet again.

"Okay…I guess I deserve that."

"Naw, you deserve way more than that," Lexi confirmed as she pulled away from his grasp folding her arms.

Kojack closed his eyes releasing a long deep breath then opened them gazing down into her perfect dark eyes, full lips, and cute nose that had now appeared humungous on her face from spreading due to the pregnancy. She stared back at him but he could tell the level of frustration she was feeling about him. It was then that he knew it would take a lot more than just some measly ass kissing to get her back to the loving way she was before with him.

"Lexi, words cannot express what I feel for you. Every time I think about you my heart gets butterflies, even when we're together. There's something about you that possesses me that I can't let go. All while I was gone I sat in this very office thinking and feeling miserable. I hated myself for what I did to you. I hated the fact that I couldn't touch you or hold you and tell you everything's gonna be alright."

"Kojack, don't…"

"Just…just hear me out first. Since I've been with you I've been happier than I've ever been. You do things and treat me way better than any other woman I've ever known."

"Oh now you consider me a woman?"

Kojack bowed his head in shame, but was determined to remain on track with his speech, "So I know that I haven't been the man you needed me to be in the past but I was wondering if starting tonight we could start anew. No games, no drama, no miscommunication, just you, me, and the baby. I know now that you are the woman for me."

Lexi shook her head in disbelief that he was saying all of these things. He never spoke like that to her not even when they got back together before. She was shocked by his willingness to put his heart on the line knowing that she was heated about the way he played her. She wanted to forgive him, take him in her arms and caress him all over until the sun came up. But she knew that if he was going to do right this time he would need to work hard for it.

"Tell me one damn thing, Kojack. Why did you leave me?" she asked attempting to lower her sizzle a bit.

"Honestly," he hesitated wondering if it would make matters worse. "After Diamond told us about her situation, I got a little spooked and needed some time to think. While I was thinking, I got a test done."

"Hmm, so you slept with Diamond?"

"NO! I mean, I don't think I did. I mean no, no."

"How in the fuck don't you know who you slept with?" she attacked.

"Oh like you do? Yeah I know about you, baby."

"First of all, yes I did my thing but I only fucked with people who meant something to me in some way or another so I could remember who I fucked. And yes I remember all of their names. I just lost my virginity two years ago and despite what you might have heard, just because I like sex, it hasn't been that many."

"Yeah?"

"Yeah, motherfucka and for the record, no you didn't sleep with Diamond. That's my sister. You think I don't know the story?"

Lexi had snapped on him so bad that all he could do was laugh. She was definitely a pistol firing round after round at him, not giving him a break for a second. It was that attitude that drew him even closer to her. He found her sassiness sexy and confident, loving how she held her ground. He could not figure out why none of this was evident to him before. Kojack felt he waited long enough and it was now or never.

"Lexi, I'm telling you all of this, not only to beg you to take me back," he said as he went around to the back of his large metal desk digging through one of the drawers, "But also to let you know that I can't live without you."

"What are you doing?"

"Something I was going to do anyway. I'm just doing it a little early," Kojack smiled as he bent down one knee, kneeling down in front of her holding up a tiny brown box.

"What is this?" Lexi asked breathing heavily, afraid to touch it.

"Open it."

She took the box from him prying the lid up revealing a small beautiful and classic diamond ring. The band was thin and gold with a perfectly raised small diamond setting. It was not comically big and even in low light it shined like the sun. Lexi was taken aback by the splendor of the ring and could barely take her eyes off of it, gasping every chance she got.

"Do you like it? It was my great grandmother's," he noted, pointing out the ring's extra sentimental value.

"It's amazing."

"Lexi, will you marry me?" Kojack proposed in his most passionate voice.

"Kojack, I don't know...what to say."

"It's so easy to say no so, just say yes," he smiled.

Lexi pulled on his arms helping him to his feet then reached up wrapping her short arms around his tall neck. His tongue became one with hers as he grabbed the back of her head massaging in a relaxing motion. Both of their temperatures rose as their hands moved about each other's bodies feeling and groping the very curves each one possessed. The heat in the room felt like it had skyrocketed in under a minute and at its peak, Lexi broke connection, slowly separating herself from him.

"I can't do this, baby," she said wiping the wetness from around her lips.

"HUH?" Kojack gasped out of breath and confused.

"I don't think this is right. We haven't

resolved anything. I don't want to let your sweet little speech and this beautiful ring influence me. How do I know for sure that when times get rough you won't just up and leave me again?"

"But I told you I won't baby. What do you want from me?"

"I want you to start living up to your fucking word. If I have this baby and you leave me then what? I'm just stuck alone with a baby, when I could have just done that on my own from jump?"

"What the hell is wrong with you bitches? A real nigga bleeds his heart for y'all and then you stomp on it claiming that's not enough!" Kojack's voice rose to an octave.

"Eh, you know, I was wondering if I was making the right decision. Now I know. I'm sorry, I gotta go."

"Where the fuck are you going Lex? I'm your ride," Kojack boasted picking up the car keys from off of his desk then tossing them back down.

"She said she can't do this, motherfucker. Didn't you hear her?" Nikki shouted as she busted through the closet doors pointing a long black revolver.

"Nikki?" Kojack shrieked, "What the fuck

are you doing in there and why the fuck you got my gun?"

"Never give a girl your keys to do your job for you, baby. She just might overstep her bounds and do something to her benefit, like make a set of keys just for her," Nikki smiled rubbing her whisking hair out of her face with a nod.

"This is not happening, right now," Kojack sighed, "What were you doing in there?

"Oh you didn't know baby? Of course not, because you're never here to run your own damn business. Yeah, I've been taking money out of your little closet safe for years and then I recalculate the paperwork so that you never know," Nikki laughed, "Isn't it funny that you've been supporting my lavish lifestyle for a while now and didn't know it and tonight I was going to clean you out and leave your sorry ass?"

"You what?" he wailed.

"Wow ain't that some shit," Lexi smirked.

"Who's this bitch, Kojack? Huh? Is this the one got you all twisted up?" Nikki churned and criticized.

She eyed Lexi sizing her up noticing her beauty and fair skin feeling a bit of jealousy overcome her. She knew that someone was holding his attention, taking it away from her but she had no idea how beautiful she was. Her hand unconsciously pointed the gun over to her wondering what would hurt Kojack worse; to kill him or the one he truly loved.

"Ay, don't point that shit at me. I'm not the one you got beef with," Lexi said holding her hands up in surrender mode.

"Nikki. Are you crazy or something? You know you going to jail girl. This ain't even you. Come on, give me the gun," Kojack said fingering her to hand it over.

"I don't think so. See you never really took the time to learn anything about me. All you cared about was what I could do for you. You're a user and a dog," Nikki replied banging her fist against the left side of her head, "ARGH! Kojack, why don't you love me? Don't you know we could have had something together? We could be so happy, you and me."

"Okay clearly you are crazier than I knew. You're confusing business with pleasure..."

"I do everything for you!" Nikki screamed at the top of her lungs slowly falling silent, "I can't believe you did this to me."

"I've done nothing to you. Don't you get it?"

"I guess licking my pussy for four hours straight and making me cum hard as hell was nothing to you. I guess banging me, tapping my uterus every time you entered me was nothing to you."

"Wait, Kojack you slept with her?" Lexi questioned pointing in her direction, agitated and shaking her head in disbelief. "And then you turn around and indirectly call me a hoe, right?"

"Baby, I didn't fuck…okay it happened one time but that was a while ago. She's just stuck on stupid. We were never together like that," he explained.

"But you told me that you loved me. You said you loved this pussy. I told you I would wait as long as you needed me to in order to get that ring but you gave it to this bitch!" Nikki snapped.

Bang! Tiny fragments of glass shattered everywhere as Kojack covered his head. Nikki had shot out the camera in the top corner of the office.

"Next time I won't miss."

"Nikki, you are not thinking right. Okay? You need to just calm down and give me the gun while you still have time to stay out of jail for this," Kojack pleaded as his heart raced from total shock.

"You can't even keep your fucking life together and you proposing marriage. I sure dodged that bullet," Lexi stated rolling her eyes away from his direction, "Look honey, I'm gonna tell it to you like this. He's not worth the cotton his balls are cuffed in. I don't want to fight so if you want him you can have him."

"Lexi, what are you doing to me here baby?" Kojack's eyes looked crossed.

"I'm giving you what you tried to take from me baby, your freedom," Lexi winked her eye as she walked over to the desk, snatching the car keys, "It'll be parked in front of your house with the keys in the ignition so if it gets stolen, I have nothing to do with that."

Nikki was not pleased with Lexi's nonchalant attitude about this serious and dangerous situation. She wanted her to be frightened and beg her for her life. She wanted her to be trembling so bad that she pissed on herself in fear. But Lexi was far from scared. Her eyes did not water and her palms were not sweaty. She was confident that she had nothing to do with that bullshit and refused to be caught up in it. However, Nikki was not willing to let her walk out of the office door alive.

"Hold up. Where do you think your ass is going?" Nikki asked licking her dark lips.

"I'm getting the fuck outta here. If you want him all to yourself, then I don't need to be here." Lexi responded.

"LEX!" Kojack hollered through his teeth distraught by her words.

"I can't let you leave little girl. You've seen too much," Nikki stated feeling the tears water her eyes, "I'm sorry but I can't."

"Yes you can and you wanna know why?" Lexi smiled soft and angelic, "Because I'm not a little girl, I'm a lady. And ladies live by a code where we keep our mouths closed."

Silence fell over the room. Lexi did not want to give Nikki enough time to go crazy on her, grabbing the door knob pushing the door open quickly never taking her eyes of the gun for a second. Nearly out the door, Kojack watched as she just stepped out of the office without care or concern for his wellbeing. His chest caved in and his heart dropped to his feet, wanting to call out to her or scream her name. He waited to see if she would at least peak back in to speak to him or send him a sign that she was lying to Nikki and was actually going to get help. But as the door closed the only thing he heard was the sound of Nikki's lips smacking together from his gaze at Lexi's departure.

"You want her don't you?" she asked softly.

"She's carrying my seed," he replied listening to the sound of his car rev up.

"You are so fucking pathetic," Nikki laughed.

"ARGH!! Give me the fucking gun!" Kojack was beyond fed up as he rushed towards her grabbing her arm vying for the pistol.

BANG! There was a slight pause then...BANG, BANG!

His eyes were open, still and fixed. Her hand was still, there was blood everywhere. The brawl was one for an action packed Steven Spielberg movie, yet it was all too real. There were tiny specks splattered on the wall, sofa and window. The silence was ghostly but as Nikki unearthed herself out from under Kojack's still warm yet dead body, she realized she only had a matter of minutes to collect all of the cash from the safe and disappear into the night.

****

As Lexi drove down the road loving the luxury of Kojack's Lexus truck, she dreaded having to give it up once she made it to his house. She decided to make her ride all the more comfortable and exciting by fiddling with the gadgets from the ceiling console to the stereo. She turned to WGCI hoping they were not full of commercials as usual. Punching the buttons wildly, she did not find the station but stumbled upon a song she remembered Diamond told her their mother used to like.

"Go on sing that song Chaka! Woo!" Lexi juked loving the smooth rhythm of music, *"Whoa, sweet thang. Don't' you know you're my everything?"*

The song dissipated, as did her excitement as the radio announcer began speaking in a very solemn voice. She was just about to turn the channel when he said something that caught her attention prompting her to turn the radio volume up almost to the max.

Authorities are saying that the shoot out on 79th and Western in between Nicky's Restaurant and McDonald's, involved a young lady, who was only identified by the ID in her pocket. She is eighteen-year-old Diamond Burden, a Chicago native, who engaged in an all-out shootout with police this evening killing one police sergeant, whose name is not being released at this time and also ending in her fatal demise. The suspect was shot in the head killing her instantly as she refused to give up when instructed by authorities. We still have yet to know what made this young lady decide to do this and why she did not surrender. No family has been found or notified as of yet but again this is breaking news and as the story unfolds we'll be able to bring you more information. Let me add that it's just truly a shame that these young folks live their lives in the fast lane but I want to send my condolences out to the family and if you are a relative of or know Diamond please come forward so we can possibly get some answers to this tragedy and give you some answers as well.

Her mouth was agape as she pulled off of the expressway turning the volume down, she could barely drive. Her brain collapsed almost unable to function wanting to run the car into ongoing traffic and end it all as large boulders of tears fell from her eyes effortlessly. She was so lost in a daze that she had not even noticed that she was pulling up in front of Kojack's house. Every fiber on her body cringed as she parked the then turned the key to the ignition and plopped back in the seat. Her breathing became erratic and her soul began to wither away like an old rose. Shock filled her face along with the feeling of nausea and numbness.

"AGHHHHHHHH!"

Lexi screamed as loud and as hard as she possibly could. Not only had she lost one sister she had lost them both and all in the same day. It proved to be more than she could bear, her body going limp with grief setting in. She knew the police would eventually find her and commence the ongoing investigation as to why she would pull such a stunt, not to mention the questions they would have when they finally discovered Pandora's body. None of it mattered, though, because whatever they asked or did it would not be enough to bring her family back. The reality of her lonesome had begun to set in and then she clenched her t-shirt tightly, nearly ripping it clean off. Her fingernails dug into her sides and chest inflicting a pain that might take away the pain she felt inside for her loss as the tears continued to flow.

She dug deeper and deeper feeling that her clothes were constricting her more snug than usual, pulling at them in a stressful temper tantrum, squeezing her eyes together roughly. Then she opened them abruptly. She remembered the life growing inside of her. Her fingers gently ran across her stomach silently apologizing for her uncanny behavior, realizing that this life was counting on her. Though still in mourning she knew that she needed to be able to deal with her grieving in a better way for the sake of her unborn child.

"Oh shit!" She exclaimed as she exited the car heading inside of the house slamming the door behind her.

Lexi hurriedly ran to the kitchen and got the suitcase that Diamond had told her to put under the sink. Her eyes focused on everything in the house scanning for something to transfer the contents to. Her legs raced to the top of the stairs and into Kojack's bedroom looking for anything she could use, becoming frustrated that there was nothing in there until she spotted a small Nike backpack in the far corner. She emptied its contents, some workout gear, and ran back down stairs to open the case. The tiny click was like music to her ears as her eyes slowly smiled since her mouth could not at the moment.

"Fifty thousand dollars," she sighed heavily as tears silently rolled down her cheeks and onto the neat stacks of cash, "Thanks sis."

As she transferred the last bit of money to

the backpack and zipped it closed, she tossed it on her back and headed back to the front door. She debated if she wanted to take a look back at the disaster that was once a part of her but as the feeling of vomit once again made itself prevalent in her throat she decided it was best to leave the past in the past, especially since she had finally got her wish. With Kojack far out of the picture, she could finally raise baby Lex on her own happily, since now she had the means to do so. Lexi stepped out on the porch trucking down the stairs and back into Kojack's car paying attention to her surroundings.

The cops would surely be looking for her and would keep her in Chicago until their whole circus fest of investigations was over. They would blast all of their findings on the news, surely making a mockery of her and her family and she just was not prepared to deal with that. Her sisters, though as dysfunctional as she was, deserved to finally rest not be put on public display. No, Lexi had decided that she would be the one to give them their dignity. Pulling away from the curb, she decided to leave the circus hanging in the balance about all the details of her family. On her way to the airport, she thought of all the good times that she, Pandora, and Diamond shared. Because at the end of the day, family though flawed, was all that mattered.

STAY UP TO DATE ON THE LATEST GOING ON WITH NICETY!

FOLLOW ME:

@NICETYCOUTURE

LIKE ME ON FACEBOOK:

.com/NICETYCOUTURE

www.nicetyzone.com

DON'T FORGET TO REVIEW!

#SUPPORTBLACKAUTHORS

#TEAMNICETY

CPSIA information can be obtained at www.ICGtesting.com
Printed in the USA
LVOW04s2130130215

427030LV00012B/133/P